Trace

SIGNIFICANT BROTHERS #4

E. DAVIES

Trace / E. Davies. – 1st ed.
ISBN: 978-1-912245-15-4

Trace

Prologue

DUSTIN

"I TOLD YOU TO MEET ME NAKED AT THE DOOR."

Dustin raised his eyebrows slowly. "You did. I ignored you, because I'd rather not flash all my neighbors."

He let the door swing shut behind tonight's hookup, regretting for just a moment that it wasn't in the guy's face. He could probably put up with him for a few minutes, which was all he needed.

The guy—Eric?—rolled his eyes. There was nothing warm or friendly about the way he shrugged his shirt off and threw it on the floor like it had offended him.

So much for "fun, friends, and Mr. Right." Clearly, Dustin wasn't a candidate for either of the latter. He tried not to take it too much to heart.

"Bedroom's this way."

Eric shook his head. "Nah. We can do it here."

Dustin swallowed a laugh as he looked around his front hallway. Narrow and pretty boring, but he did have a nearly-empty table near the door for his keys, a change bowl, and the mail. "If that floats your boat, sure."

"Door's closed. Get your pants down," Eric told him, shrugging off his shirt to show off the rows of abs that had drawn Dustin to his profile picture.

Dustin often had his share of no-strings-attached Grindr dates, but usually with guys who had boring or blank profiles. Eric had had two entire paragraphs. He'd looked interesting… but that personality wasn't on display tonight.

Then again, he and Eric had only messaged briefly. He ought to have known by now that that meant he was just tonight's distraction, not potential for the *friends* or *Mr. Right* or any kind of future. Dustin shrugged off his disappointment at the same time as his shirt, then dropped his pants.

I don't care if you don't, he decided with a smile to himself. It was going to be an easy fuck, and it had been a while for him.

Trying not to think about the smiles on the faces of his friends in stupid long-term relationships with sex *and* romance *and* engagement rings *and* houses together, he reminded himself once again that he had to be practical. If he didn't settle for what he could get, he might never get any.

So he sank to his knees as Mr. Tonight pulled his cock out, fishing a condom out of his pocket as Eric stepped out of the last of his clothes.

"You sure?" Eric asked, shifting from foot to foot, stroking himself. He was already hard and pink in his own hand.

Dustin smirked up at him. "Yeah." He rolled it on with his mouth, mentally sighing at the latex taste.

The guy wasn't even a moaner, but one of those weird, guttural grunters. Maybe it made him feel manlier to snort and kick the ground while he got his dick sucked. Whatever —Dustin didn't care, as long as he got what he was here for.

The thickness in his mouth was pleasant enough. Dustin had always liked sucking cock, and he lost his thoughts for a few minutes as he bobbed his head, swirled his tongue firmly around the head, sucked his cheeks in, stroked the guy's balls...

"Show me your hole." Eric's voice sounded strained.

Dustin scrambled to his feet and bent over the table, licking his fingers and slowly working them inside himself.

And then Eric was moaning behind him in sharp sounds, and he felt... was that wetness across his lower back?

He glanced back. It was. Asshole hadn't even lasted long enough to get inside him. Letting his fingers slide out, he grabbed tissues to clean up, sighing audibly. He wasn't gonna embarrass the guy, but goddamn, some self-control was not uncalled-for.

"You weren't supposed to suck me off, man," Eric had the balls to complain as he shoved himself back into his pants and put his shirt on.

Dustin eyed him. "You weren't supposed to come on me without asking, either."

Eric grunted. "Sure. Cool. See ya." With that, Eric was gone.

At last, even though his cock was half-hard and aching for some kind of attention, Dustin saw the humor of the situation. No wonder Eric wanted his dates to be nude at the door, so he didn't waste a second. If he'd had the balls to say it was a choice between sucking or fucking for three minutes, they could have made the best of it. Dustin was easygoing. There were options.

This was gonna make a hell of a story to tell his friends. Dustin sank to the floor and laughed. He rolled his head back against the leg of the table with a rueful sigh when he finally caught his breath.

"Guess I'm going to the bar tonight."

CHAPTER

One

LEO

"Now, before I hand back last week's assignment, I have some general comments to make."

Years of military service helped Leo school his expression instead of rolling his eyes. This was at least the third time this semester they'd gotten this lecture, and he already knew what was coming.

Out in the real world, there's no margin for error.

On a stupid geography paper about volcanoes. It wasn't even like any of them were going to become volcano scientists—volcanists? Vulcans?—and risk wiping out some rare indigenous species of parrot if they typed the wrong date.

This was one of those people who'd gotten a little too much power and a little too comfortable with it. Surrounded by sixty eighteen-year-olds and no more than a handful of sophomores, juniors, or even seniors, the temptation to talk down to them was apparently hard to ignore.

Leo was lucky he looked young. He seemed to blend in with the rest of them, enough that he didn't get stared at like some of the "mature students" on campus. And everyone knew a few military guys who were going back to school on the VA's dime. As he'd been told, there was a general atmosphere of support, but… isolation.

Even the warning that he might feel isolated hadn't prepared him for the reality of being surrounded by kids who couldn't seem to do their own laundry or change their oil, let alone survive a war zone.

Taking a mix of evening and daytime courses for the first semester had seemed like a good idea at the time. Now he was starting to wish he'd gone for just the evening courses.

He jolted to life when the clattering chaos of students rushing out of the classroom began. The ability to tune out lectures wasn't a military thing; that had been a lifelong ability, much to the frustration of his superiors sometimes.

"Leo. Can you wait for a minute?"

Leo blinked at Professor Park, his paper clutched awkwardly in one hand as he balanced the laptop under his other arm. "Um, sure."

He stepped aside with the professor as other students claimed their papers, immediately sweating. Had his been that bad? He was pretty sure he'd just spotted an A on his paper.

"I wanted to ask where you got your sources. I know I didn't ask for a bibliography, but there were some interesting facts about desert biomes."

"I lived in the desert for a few years."

"Ah. You're one of our VA kids, aren't you?" Professor Park nodded at him when he nodded. "Thank you for your service, Leo." He clearly felt pleased with himself for saying it and waited for a response.

Leo swallowed the groan of frustration. If that was all he wanted to say, he could have complimented his own generous patriotic spirit in the mirror and saved Leo the time. He had his own job to get to. "My pleasure. So I'm not in trouble?"

"Oh, no. That explains everything. I was impressed with your work. Diligent and high-quality."

"Thanks. Sorry to run, though. I have to get to work. See you next class, sir." Leo waved slightly and jogged out of the classroom, then broke into a sprint as he headed for the car.

Only when he got to his car and fumbled to unlock the door did he remember why he hadn't been in more of a rush to get out of the house with a packed supper for later.

He wasn't even working today.

He thumped his forehead and climbed into his car. Classes were the only thing helping him remember the days of the week.

Now he regretted racing out of the classroom. Other students lingered, chatted, made friends, got coffee together… and he was always rushing to work or to sit alone at home.

Leo drew a calming breath and let it out to focus on the drive home. The routine was nice, but dissatisfaction still stirred in his stomach as he walked through the front door of his quiet little apartment.

He hadn't expected to be so lonely without the structure of his days—and his were some of the least structured of any of his friends in the military. Photographers were ready to shoot when needed, as needed, in a whole different way.

Again, Leo's gaze wandered to his camera.

He used police department-issued gear for his current job, and he hadn't picked his own up often over the last few months. Moving back here had taken its toll on him, but he'd never expected reintegration to be this difficult.

He had a new job he liked, and which helped him bring some good into this world—if only by catching evil bastards.

But what about friends?

That made up his mind: he'd hit up the bars. Wander around downtown, see what had changed in the last few years. Knoxville looked different now, even with just a few years having gone by.

Time to act normal, just for a night.

CHAPTER
Two

DUSTIN

"AND WHAT'S A FINE YOUNG MAN LIKE YOURSELF DOING HERE all by yourself?"

The man by Dustin's side had a classic Texan drawl, a giant belt buckle, and a hand that was creeping down Dustin's back toward his ass.

It wasn't like Dustin thought he was too good for him. A Tennessee boy himself, Dustin had never liked anyone who judged people on where they came from.

More bothersome was the hand, which was now at his lower back and not showing any sign of stopping, and the oily attitude.

Dustin reached behind himself to lace his fingers with the guy's and turned to face him, making a pretense of flirting. "Waiting for a nice gentleman to come along."

"Well, ain't it lucky for you I'm here tonight?"

"Not particularly." Dustin pirouetted out of the hold and deposited the hand neatly on the bar top with a grimace reserved for the worst of his forensic slides.

The other guy stared for a moment, his bushy brows

pushed together like he couldn't work out what was going on. "Well, you're a sassy little thing."

Dustin was used to it. He was unmistakably a twink, in the eyes of the guys cruising here at one of the few gay bars in Knoxville. He couldn't avoid it, so he worked with it. Between his work clothes and subtle blond highlights, he screamed *nerdy twink* from across the room.

Unfortunately, a lot of big, hunky cowboys took that as an invitation to the party in his pants without even asking first.

"I'm going to sass somewhere else in a minute. I suggest you do the same."

The guy leered and stepped close again, but before he could touch Dustin's back, another hunk had shouldered his way between them.

"Pardon me, I think the next dance was mine." The twang threaded through the deep voice told Dustin it was another local boy coming to his rescue.

Dustin took the chance to look him over: broad shoulders, a bright boyish smile, and hazel eyes he could get lost in. He was handsome but not a showoff—a boy next door type, only with way more muscles. His shirt made them obvious, but Dustin tried not to be too obvious himself as he noticed them.

Clearly defeated, the first guy left at last, muttering under his breath.

Dustin's lip quirked as he glanced up at the newcomer. Sweet, if unnecessary, to come to his defense. "And what do *you* charge?" He looked surprised, so Dustin grinned and added, "For protection. Not an hourly rate. I'm kinda broke this week."

The new guy laughed. "Damn. I was hoping I was hot enough to charge."

"Oh, I say you are." Dustin appreciated the broad shoulders barely hidden by his t-shirt, the way it clung to his body. He could see pecs and guess at abs. And he was gorgeous, too. The kind of guy he'd never expect to take an interest in him for more than a night. "Take the compliment."

"Is this where I say *I charge a kiss* and then try some cheesy pickup line?" He shrugged easily. "Don't worry about it. He looked like a creep." His eyes sharpened with interest, though, as he met Dustin's gaze. "But, uh…"

Hope lifted Dustin's heart. Some big protector swooping in to rescue him from a dick at the bar *was* kind of embarrassingly hot.

"But?" Dustin teased, trying not to seem overeager.

He didn't seem in a rush to take Dustin home. He settled onto the stool next to Dustin instead. "What brings you here?"

"The worst Grindr hookup ever—no, in a while." Dustin grinned. "*Ever* is a pretty high bar. Or low."

"Right, right. So, I'm going to seem like the least observant guy in the world in a few moments."

Dustin cocked his head. "How so?"

"This is a gay bar?"

"Um." Dustin wasn't sure whether to laugh or stare. It seemed fairly obvious to him. "Yeah?"

"Ah." The other guy just laughed. "That explains, well… everything."

Dustin's heart sank. "You're not straight, are you?"

"Sorry. I have this secret I have to tell you." The guy's eyes twinkled. If he was telling the truth, it was really unfair that he had dimples so perfectly formed. "I'm flattered, though."

"Not, uh…" Dustin couldn't think of a word other than *repulsed* or *terrified*. "Offended?"

"It's hard to hurt my feelings if you try. Complimenting me sure as hell ain't gonna do it. I'm Leo, by the way."

Dustin burst out laughing. "Good point." Weirdly, though he'd come here without the idea of friendship or romance in mind at all, there was something drawing him toward this guy—a curiosity, for lack of a better word.

Not to mention the sparks when they shook hands. The warm, broad palm against his felt *good*, and it was hard to pull away.

Today was the weirdest day in living memory. "Dustin. Uh, so… how did you end up here?"

"I just moved back to town around Christmas after a few years away," Leo told him. "I've been wandering around the places I used to like. Didn't pay much attention to the signs… or the rainbow flag in the window… Apparently this one got gayer while I was away."

Dustin grinned. "Sorry. We take over and fix failing businesses."

"And redecorate, apparently. That stereotype isn't totally wrong." Leo looked around. "The place looks a lot nicer now."

"You say that, but you haven't seen some of my single brothers' places," Dustin laughed.

"You have gay brothers?"

"Best friends. We call each other brothers," Dustin explained. It was the simplest way of putting it.

Leo seemed to instantly understand. "That's cool. So, you came here to pick up someone like me, huh? Sorry I wasn't what you were hoping for."

"Me too," Dustin agreed, winking at Leo. He was actually

comfortable joking around with the guy, seeing how at ease he was. "That could have been fun."

Remarkably at ease, for a straight guy. A straight guy who gave him a quick up-and-down glance, for that matter.

"I'd better get going soon, though," Leo said, glancing at his watch. "I've got work tomorrow."

Uh oh. The thrill of the chase set in, and Dustin couldn't shake the thought once he'd had it. Who *didn't* want to tempt a straight guy? Unless Leo was bi. He hadn't actually asked. That was a thrilling possibility.

"If you wanna hang out sometime, by any definition, I'll give you my number." Dustin grinned and tilted his head slightly to make his meaning clear. It was worth a shot. "I could use more friends and fun in my life."

Leo looked flustered for a moment. It was an adorable look on a man who was essentially a brick wall of muscle. "Oh! Uh, sure. Yeah." He fumbled with his phone and handed it over.

Dustin entered his name and number and grinned, handing it back. "There. In case you need anyone to point out the gay bars next time."

"It worked out okay for us both this time," Leo said, grinning. "If that asshole comes back, tell him I'm your boyfriend or something."

"I'd be thrilled to," Dustin teased. "Thanks for the out." He tried his luck and leaned in for a lingering hug, letting his arms wrap around Leo's shoulders. "I appreciate it," he murmured.

Leo seemed startled for a moment, but then he responded, those strong arms closing around him with an awkward back-pat to boot. *So straight,* Dustin thought, trying not to laugh. "Of course."

But Dustin noticed he didn't let go until Dustin loosened his grip and leaned back again. The sparks that flashed through Dustin's body were impossible to ignore. He could already picture himself being wrapped up by those arms with his back against the mattress…

Whoa. Cool it, he told himself, crossing his legs.

"See you around." Leo sounded and even looked a little dazed as he slid his glass over the bar and stood up.

Dustin bit back a smile. Whether he knew it or not, Leo was showing signs of interest. Maybe that phone number in his address book would be a baited hook for later. Hopefully *soon*-later. "Bye."

Strangely enough, he didn't feel like hanging out here and fishing for another nibble. Maybe because he'd had a conversation with a guy who was interested in more than his ass. Whatever the case, Dustin's sexual frustration from Mr. Earlier—Earl or whatever the hell his name was—had passed.

He'd just call it a weird day and head home, definitely not thinking about Leo's biceps flexing against his shoulders and those narrow, muscled hips thrusting against his.

Cool it, cowboy. Dustin subtly adjusted himself as he stood up and quickly shrugged his coat on to leave.

Straight guys only went gay in fantasies and porn. He might as well daydream about it, but in reality? He knew he didn't stand a chance. Unless Leo's subtle signs of interest *did* mean more.

But he couldn't count on that.

CHAPTER
Three

LEO

Okay. That was weird.

It was only a few degrees below freezing in Knoxville. That was pretty damn good for January. The downside? The chill wasn't enough to sweep the hot flush from Leo's cheeks.

Leo leaned against the wall and looked around casually, as if waiting for someone. His heart was still thudding, and his skin itched like someone had suddenly connected bundles of nerves that he hadn't been aware of before now.

Was that chemistry? Okay, it was. Obviously. There was no denying it—just like everyone said they knew it when they felt it. *But for a guy?*

It kind of made sense, when he thought about it. While his peers had been chasing girls and getting their hearts broken, he'd been able to ignore that scene and pour his energy into school, then his career.

Leo had gone on dates with women. He'd tried the whole dating scene more than once, but things had always fizzled out before getting to bed. He'd always figured it was his own fault, that he didn't know what he was doing or wasn't trying hard enough.

And it wasn't that he *wasn't* attracted to them. He was still convinced he hadn't been wrong in his assessment at the time. He'd decided he'd been talking to the wrong women. It had never been the fact that they were women that had killed the spark.

He'd never really considered looking at guys that way, too. Now everything was starting to make sense, though. He'd had sparks with men before—but he'd thought he just idolized them, or thought they were great buddies.

Goddamn. This was a hell of a lot of self-realization for a Knoxville sidewalk.

Leo tried to convince himself he was going home, or at least to another bar nearby to have a drink and steady his nerves.

But his gut instinct was telling him to do neither, and his body was humming with nervous energy.

Go after him. Find out what this is.

It wasn't even the usual exasperation and frustration with being a virgin after all these years—how many other guys his age were? None, he was pretty sure.

This time, it wasn't ego telling him to just try it. Maybe that was why he finally listened to that voice and turned around to shoulder his way through the bar door again.

His heart raced. It felt like a mission—like he was walking into another combat zone, armed with only his camera against God only knew what. He was underprepared and overconfident all over again, following gut instinct as much as his training to keep him safe.

If photography had taught him one thing, it was to grab

the moment while it was there. So many shots he regretted not taking—far more than the few he regretted taking.

Dustin wasn't going to be one of those shots.

"Hey." He approached Dustin from behind and gently placed a hand on his shoulder, hoping his nervousness didn't show on his face. He was already wearing his jacket—had he met another guy? Already?

Dustin whirled to face him. "Whoa. That was quick." There was a bright hope shining in his eyes. Gorgeous, even when he wasn't giving Leo this perfect smile. They were a warm, light brown, and strangely enchanting. He had his hair spiked up with light highlights sprinkled throughout that brought out the warmth of his eyes. And his smile—shy at first, but showing unrestrained joy when he was amused. Dimples? Those sealed the deal.

Leo tried for a coy smile in return. "Yeah. Well, I didn't wanna risk not getting through on the phone."

"Yeah?" Dustin already leaned against the bar, looking like he was ready to go home already. "Have you changed your mind on the fees for your services?"

Leo swallowed hard, then nodded. "Yeah. Yeah, if you want. Were you about to go?"

"Well, you just made my night all over again. I'll see what I can do in return." Dustin winked. "I was about to leave. On my own. I'd rather not."

"Leave? Or… on your own?"

"I'd rather take you home," Dustin told him, and then Dustin's hand was on Leo's waist. "In my experience, labels don't have to matter."

Leo nodded slowly, jerkily. No way of explaining the thought process that had just been running through his head.

Besides, Dustin had a good way of putting it. "Yeah. Exactly. I care more about… the experience."

Dustin gave him a bright smile. "Yeah. Me, too. And you can't be worse than my Grindr date."

"You'll have to tell me about that on the way to your place," Leo told him, raising a brow.

Dustin grinned and dug out his phone, opening an app to call them a car. "Yeah. It's not much of a story, but… it's a weird one."

Okay. Success, step one. Leo straightened up and leaned casually on the counter, his cheeks flushed. He could do this. Now he had to get Dustin home, and get his clothes off, and… figure out the rest from there.

"It was nothing exciting," Dustin told him as they waited outside. He leaned into Leo slightly, wrapping his arm around Leo's waist tentatively.

Leo let him lean there and put his hand on Dustin's back. It felt a bit weird, but just unfamiliar. "Yeah? I was under the impression Grindr dates were supposed to be exciting."

"Supposed to be," Dustin told him with a laugh. "It's a mixed bag. This guy turned out to last about five minutes, including the time it took to get his clothes off. I sucked him off, and he was gonna fuck me, but he just came on me instead."

"Didn't even get the tip in?" Leo laughed, his arm tightening around Dustin's waist. If that was the bar, he was confident he could step over it.

Dustin groaned. "Nope. If he'd told me, I wouldn't have sucked him off *quite* so well." He cast Leo an unmissable sideways glance. "But I'm too good for my own good, apparently."

"I bet you are," Leo murmured. The car pulled up and

interrupted them, which was just as well, because Leo was trying to figure out how dirty they should talk in public. "After you." He opened the car door for Dustin.

The car ride was mercifully quick, because Leo found his tongue tied the whole time. Like a goddamn teenager, but an adult who was supposed to know how all of this worked by now. Instinct could take over in the bedroom. It was everything around it that he didn't know yet.

But Dustin didn't seem to notice if he was awkward. He talked about the development of Knoxville over the last few years until they got to his house, and then led Leo toward the door.

This is it. The car was gone, and Leo was really fucking in over his head now. He followed Dustin into the place.

His first impression was that it was cute. Very homey, down to the little table by the door for keys and change. The walls were painted light, airy colors, and there were a few pieces of art in the hallway. It all fit his impression of Dustin so far.

Dustin was turning to him now, kicking his shoes off.

Shit. Right. Hooking up. Leo wanted to touch Dustin again, wrap his arms around him and feel the way he fit perfectly against his chest. So he shrugged off his jacket and tossed it aside, toed off his shoes, and did just that.

Dustin leaned into him, his hands running slowly up Leo's back to cup the back of his head.

It happened so naturally: Leo pulled Dustin firmly against him, their bodies hot and hard together, and their lips met.

It was a warm, sensual, slow kiss that promised so much more. Dustin's lips were soft and delicious. He tilted his head slightly, his tongue lapping gently at Leo's lips until Leo gasped for breath.

Dustin's hands squeezed Leo's ass, making him almost jump with surprise, and then Dustin laughed. "You have a great ass. I've been waiting to do that," he murmured against Leo's lips.

Leo grinned. "Naughty," he murmured. "Yet you look so sweet."

"Oh, I am. And I bet your cock will be in my mouth, too."

Leo ground against Dustin's thigh, his hands sliding down to the curve of Dustin's ass. "Got a bedroom around here anywhere?"

"I sure do." Dustin hooked a finger into Leo's belt near the buckle, maddeningly close to the bulge in Leo's jeans.

Leo followed as he was led to a room off the hallway—again, it was small, airy, and cozy. "Nice place."

"Thanks." Dustin kicked the door shut and pressed Leo up against the door. Those sweet brown eyes were hungry. He looked like he'd been waiting all night for this. To be fair, the poor guy had.

Leo wanted to make it good for him. "What do you want? Other than me in your sweet little ass? Where do you wanna start?" *God, let me not sound like a newbie now.*

But Dustin's lips parted for a moment, his mouth hanging open. He wasn't laughing. In fact, he looked turned on. He gulped, and then his lips tugged up into a smile. "Oh. I don't usually get asked that."

"Is there a format for a standard Grindr date?"

"Pretty much," Dustin grinned.

Leo was overcome by curiosity. It was more than a scientific interest now, he had to admit. With a man's body against his, he found himself suddenly hungry for any bit of information he could get. "Do you ever just wanna skip straight to the sex? Or do they always do that, and you want foreplay?"

"I've been waiting for a good fuck all evening." Dustin moaned and leaned in for another kiss.

Leo kissed Dustin thoroughly, sucking gently on his lower lip until his knees went weak, then grabbing him to steady him as he kissed him a little more. Finally, he pushed Dustin's chest to steer him over to the bed.

His cock was painfully hard in his jeans. This was nothing like porn. Fuck, this was a hundred times better. His brain was spinning with ideas, and he hardly knew where he wanted to start.

I'm probably bad at giving oral, Leo reasoned. *But he said he was good.* "I want to see more of you."

Dustin sat on the edge of the bed and pulled his shirt off in one fluid movement. "Like that?"

Leo gulped, still standing by the edge of the bed as he stared down at the gorgeous, lithe man who was sitting at crotch-level. "Yeah. Yeah, like that," he murmured.

Dustin wriggled closer to him, grabbing his hips and pulling him in until he buried his face in Leo's crotch, kissing the bulge. "Your shirt now."

Leo fought the fabric of his sweater and shirt off over his head at once, dumping the clothes on the floor. Dustin's eyes widened and scanned his torso, then slowly raked up to his face. "You like it?"

"You're fucking ripped. Of course I like it," Dustin grinned, his hands running up Leo's stomach and chest.

Holy fuck, that felt good! Leo's hips jolted as Dustin's lips provided light pressure to his shaft through his jeans. Sparks were flying now, his breath coming in short and quick gasps as Dustin's hands explored his body.

"You're gorgeous," Leo breathed out. Watching Dustin kiss him with the promise of something to come was incredible. He wanted to memorize the sight. It was so hard not to express every ounce of his awed appreciation.

How the fuck had he lived without this?

Dustin grinned, popping Leo's belt buckle open with an expert hand and pulling his jeans off. He had Leo's hard cock in his hand within moments, gently teasing the underside with his palm.

Oh, fuck. He's good.

Leo's cheeks flushed as he tried not to compare his inexperience against Dustin's clear knowledge of what he was doing. He moaned loudly as Dustin's hand stroked down his shaft, rolling a condom down it, followed immediately by the wet heat of his mouth.

"Oh, fuck," Leo whispered. "I see why the other guy... had the problems he did." Dustin's mouth provided the perfect suction around him, his hand tight around the base of his shaft while his tongue played with the head of his cock.

Dustin moaned around his cock, and the vibrations sent an extra chill of pleasure through him.

"God, that's good." The pretty pink lips stretched around his cock, his eyes flickering up his body to meet his gaze...

Just relaxing and letting the other man make him feel good was heavenly. Leo was going to need to feel this again.

If this is his idea of friendship, I could do that.

Was Leo the kind of guy to have a friend with benefits? Hell, yeah. He was now. He'd clearly had his head stuck in the sand all this time.

"You're beautiful," Leo whispered, running his hand across Dustin's hair and ruffling it gently.

He had never really stopped to think about why he found some men gorgeous. He'd assumed it was a jealous admiration from afar. But maybe he'd wanted to admire them from a lot closer.

Fuck. It was like discovering a puzzle piece he'd never known had been missing.

Dustin slowly pulled his head up the shaft, lapping under the head a few more times as he fumbled with his own pants.

Leo shook his head and gripped Dustin by the elbows to raise him to his feet, then changed his mind. He wanted Dustin on his back. "Lie down."

"Oooh. Yes, sir," Dustin teased, scooting backward on the bed as Leo chased on hands and knees. They were both laughing by the time Dustin reached the pillow and Leo pinned him down, straddling him.

"I want you. You got lube?" Leo asked.

Fuck. He hadn't thought this part out, either. In theory, he knew how to finger someone else. And who hadn't tried it on themselves sooner or later? His own attempts had been pleasurable but clumsy.

Dustin grinned and jerked his head toward the bedside table. A bottle of lube already sat there.

"Oh. Prepared. Well done," Leo praised with a grin.

"Thanks." Dustin winked. "I didn't want to wait a second longer than I had to wait to feel your cock deep in me."

Leo's whole body shuddered with arousal, his cock stiff and aching for stimulation again. He ground against Dustin's hip a few times as he leaned over to grab the lube.

"Let me," Dustin murmured, plucking the tube from him and slicking his fingers. Before Leo could even protest, Dustin slid his fingers into himself, his head rolling back against the pillow.

Leo closed a hand around his cock, willing himself not to come on the spot. Dustin's face was taut with pleasure, his body rippling and back arching off the bed as his fingers slid into his tight hole. The moaning sound he made was obscene.

"I could watch that all day," Leo growled, his voice rough with need.

Dustin smiled for a second but shook his head. "Not tonight. Tonight, you fuck me."

"*Yes*," Leo whispered, waiting for Dustin to give the word. He'd never wanted anything so badly in his life. It took every ounce of self-control not to pounce on the man and press kisses all over his body, drink in the taste and smell of him…

A minute later, Dustin spread his legs and cocked his head, gazing at Leo again, his expression pleading.

That was a need Leo could fill. He crouched over Dustin and braced himself on one forearm, cupping Dustin's cheek with his other hand. He took a moment to kiss him slowly and deeply.

Dustin moaned against his lips, his hands wrapping around the back of Leo's head. His kiss was hard, his teeth grazing against sensitive skin.

Already hot with desire, the burn under Leo's skin intensified to a roaring fire of need. He growled quietly, his hand sliding to his cock to guide himself inside.

Instinct took him a long way, and common sense did the rest. He took it slowly as he pushed into the almost unbearably hot, tight hole. He fit perfectly, rings of muscle closing around his shaft and swallowing him deep as he pushed in.

"Fuck! Yes," Leo panted, and Dustin pressed little kisses along his mouth. He was sweating already, his breathing fast. "Oh, that's good. Tell me if it's too much." Leo's shaft slid all the way inside, and he pulled his hips back slowly, testing the waters.

"You feel good," Dustin reassured him, his quick breaths evening out again. "Oh, *yes*. That's what I was waiting for."

Leo couldn't explain the feelings surging through him: he was possessive, protective, and aroused to the very bone. *Mine*, was the only thing he could think. *Mine, and I'm going to make him feel so good.*

He tried to keep his movements slow, angling his hips to keep his shaft lined up right. "You're fucking sexy. I'm glad that other asshole didn't keep you at home tonight."

"Me, too." Dustin was breathtakingly beautiful right now, and everything just... felt right. A light switch had been flipped on in his brain. There was no going back now.

As Dustin tugged on his hips and panted, "More," Leo was more than happy to fulfill that desire.

"Fuck me. Hard, baby."

The pet name made Leo's cheeks burn. He pushed the feeling aside to figure out later and kissed Dustin hard, letting his steady rhythm speed up. Once he had the hang of it, it was easy and all too fucking good.

Leo was pounding Dustin into the mattress within minutes, his hands rising to grab Dustin's and lace their fingers together above Dustin's head.

"Yes!" Dustin panted, rolling his head back.

Leo ducked his head to lick and kiss at Dustin's exposed throat and jaw. He found a spot near Dustin's ear that made him squirm adorably—and in a way that ground their bodies together wonderfully.

Oh, right. He's gonna want to come, too. Leo let go of one of Dustin's hands and braced himself on his elbow to slip a hand between them. The moment he caressed that aroused cock with a tight fist, Dustin bucked against him.

"Fuck!"

"Sorry," Leo gasped, loosening the grip.

"N-No, do it again. I'm ready now," Dustin moaned. "Please."

Leo gradually squeezed tighter while he stroked hard and fast. He tried to match the pace of his hips. He could feel Dustin quivering and clenching around him as he did so, growing closer to the edge.

Just as well, because his own balls were drawing tight, his shaft swelling. If Dustin didn't hurry…

"Yes!" Dustin bucked under him, grabbing Leo hard as his nails dug into Leo's back. They were both going to be sticky now, but Leo loved that, too.

Dustin squeezed tight around Leo's sensitive shaft, and that was enough. Leo came hard, gasping Dustin's name as his thrusts became quick and erratic. "Yes! Oh my… fuck… Dustin…"

"Gorgeous," Dustin whispered, his touch gentler now as he smoothed his hands up and down Leo's back. "I think I scratched you. Hope that's okay."

Leo started laughing as he slid out, awareness of the rest of the world slowly returning to him. "That's… yeah, that's fine. *Fine*. A hundred percent."

Dustin grinned. "Side effect of being well-fucked."

I did a good job. Leo's ego responded to that and his chest swelled, making Dustin laugh. He rolled onto his side slowly as it all started to sink in. He'd just had sex with a man and it had been fucking wonderful.

"I'm… wow." Leo slowly pulled the condom off and looked around for a trash can, then found tissues to give him something to do while it sank in.

When he looked back at Dustin, the slender, gorgeous young man was sprawled across the bed in a way that made

Leo want to touch him. Just caress those ribs, run a thumb along the small nipples, cup his hip, pull him in for a kiss…

Shit. I think I'm hooked. "So, I can keep your number?" Leo asked. He grinned ruefully. "Not to sound, uh, too eager."

"No such thing as too eager," Dustin murmured, his hand closing around Leo's wrist. He pulled his hand toward him and kissed the palm in a gesture that made Leo's heart melt. "Please do."

Okay. He could do this.

"Or you could stick around for round two." Dustin smirked and waggled his eyebrows.

"I really *do* have work," Leo murmured, reluctantly pulling back from Dustin. It was true, he did—and a little thinking to do, besides.

He'd managed to impress and satisfy Dustin once. Could he do it again? How the hell was he going to learn to suck cock? What if Dustin wanted, like, a label? Was he opposed to that? He didn't think so. Why not?

Dustin's gaze flickered over his face. Instead of asking, though, Dustin just nodded. "Fair enough. Keep my number, though."

"Oh, I will." Leo slowly searched for his clothes and pulled them back on, one piece at a time. His body was sluggish and lazy and deeply satisfied.

Dustin hummed under his breath and pushed himself to sit up against the headboard. Then he followed Leo to the door, still casually naked. "Thanks for that. That was a million times better than earlier."

"Glad to help. You weren't bad yourself," Leo grinned, shrugging on his jacket and awkwardly pulling his shoes on.

He straightened up. This was the awkward moment. Did they kiss goodbye?

Leo hesitated on the doorstep, the door half-open as Dustin ducked behind it and out of view of the street. *If in doubt, probably better not.* "Good night," he settled on and raised his hand in a quick wave.

"Night," Dustin wished him, and the door clicked shut.

Then he was striding down the street through the cold. It was a long walk, but he knew his way back from here. He could really use the fresh air to cool off and try to get his thoughts straight. If not *straight.*

Leo's lips stretched in a smile—small at first, then bigger.

He'd just had sex, and it was *awesome.*

If only he had someone to brag to without sounding like a total loser.

Hey, guys. Sex is awesome. By the way, I'm not straight. Who knew?

Leo burst out laughing and broke into a lighthearted jog, skipping over the curbs. He didn't care how weird he looked. For now, he didn't even care what was going to happen. His heart had led him the right way, and listening to it had paid off.

What the hell? Might as well make sure Dustin had his number, too. Leo pulled out his phone and sent a quick text. It felt like the courteous thing to do.

That was great. Thanks. Good night :)

As he pocketed his phone, Leo started humming a nonsense tune. For the first time in a long time, he felt good through and through.

CHAPTER
Four

DUSTIN

"No way. Knoxville isn't that small."

Dustin stared doubtfully at the collection of photos and forensic reports from the investigators on scene. Among them all, he couldn't help but notice one signature: unmistakably *Leo*.

It was a simple case: break and enter, but they'd found a few trace materials on the scene. The lead investigator was even sure he knew who did it. It was Dustin's job to figure out if they were indeed fibers from their suspect's shirt.

Sometimes he could tell after one glance at the tiny strands that their working theory was shit. His colleagues always hoped that things would be easy, and it was often his job to screw up their hypothesis, which didn't always make him popular.

But the photographer's name… Leo?

Dustin's curiosity was itching terribly. Even by the time he'd finished cataloguing the last of the materials found on scene—white cotton fibers consistent with a thick sweater like the victims' son had been wearing the night before—he couldn't stop wondering.

"Got good news for me?" That was Jonathon, the lead investigator on this one, anxiously ducking into the lab. They always wanted things done twice as fast as possible, with half as much trace evidence as was ideal.

"Good for you, bad for your perp. The fibers were thick, white cotton. The photographer caught them on the broken window, right?"

"Yeah. And a few more on the floor."

"Where exactly?" Dustin dropped into his rolling chair and flipped through the photos in the file. "Ah, there we are. On top of the glass."

"So there's no way it was left over from their fight the night before." Jonathon pumped his fist. "I knew it."

"The red powder is definitely a kind of paint from whatever was used to break the window. A hammer?" Dustin guessed. "I want to double-check where that was found. Is, uh, Leo in?"

"The new guy? Yeah, I think he's here for a few more hours. I'll grab him."

Jonathon was gone, leaving Dustin barely enough time to prepare himself before Leo was walking into the room, Jonathon by his side.

One and the same.

"You had some questions?" The question died on Leo's lips as he caught sight of Dustin, his eyes widening. "Oh, hey. Dustin."

Dustin was feeling the same way. How the hell hadn't he noticed this man before? And why hadn't he recognized him last night? "Leo," he greeted with a courteous nod, trying not to let his surprise register. Jonathan was right *there*, after all.

"I don't think we've met here."

"No." Leo's lip quirked into a half-smile, reminding Dustin of the way he'd kissed him so thoroughly last night.

Fuck. He wasn't lying about having to go to work.

"I think my shifts hadn't lined up with yours yet."

"Must be that," Dustin agreed.

"So," Jonathon interrupted, clearly impatient, "the paint flecks."

"Right."

Dustin could almost—*almost*—forget last night's activities with his mind on work. He bounced around theories with them for a minute, double-checking that Leo had captured photos of the location of the paint fleck-dusted shard before they'd collected it for him.

Leo seemed almost offended. "Of course."

"Then it's watertight." Jonathon nodded to himself. "We just gotta find the hammer, or whatever it was. Crowbar? Can you tell me what brand of paint those flecks are?"

Dustin gave him an icy look. "If you find me a tool, I can test it for a match. I don't do color matching for living rooms or thieves' tools."

Leo choked back a noise of amusement, and Jonathon looked embarrassed for a moment. "Oh. Yeah," Jonathon quickly muttered.

"I'd check the hardware stores nearby," Dustin suggested. "Those are red flecks. Look for red tools."

"And their garage, of course. Could have stolen something and returned it afterward..." Jonathon wandered out of the room, muttering to himself.

Leo glanced between the now-empty doorway and Dustin, and then laughed. "Good job, detective."

"It's my job." Dustin shrugged and cleared his throat. "Sorry for asking about the photos earlier."

"Nah. It's okay. I *am* new," Leo shook his head. "But you can count on me."

Dustin gave him a quick, secretive smile. "I hope so."

Leo cleared his throat. "I like your... attention to detail." He gestured around. "I didn't know... I mean, it fits. It's cool. Good work. Not that you need my praise. I better make sure I'm not neglecting mine, hah. See you around."

With that, he strode out, leaving Dustin blinking and staring after him. No sign of Jonathon returning, either.

"Men," Dustin concluded after a few moments. Typical. Got what they needed and left. He was still trying not to smile as he looked at the doorway again.

Enough time wasted on men, anyway. He pulled the photos toward himself and paged through them again.

Leo had an eye for detail himself, and clearly good training: the photos were properly exposed, the depth of field was as broad as possible, and every piece of evidence was meticulously catalogued.

That kind of eye for detail *was* hot.

But why run away so fast? Maybe Leo was struggling with his own attraction. He had strongly implied he wasn't gay at the bar, but he'd certainly been good in bed.

Could this be a thing? Or become one?

Dustin sank into a chair, pulling his keyboard closer. He had a report to type up. He didn't have time to be daydreaming.

It didn't stop the series of thoughts occurring to him: dating coworkers was never a good idea. Hookups never became real relationships in his experience. And in any case, a forensics guy was not the kind of man his family wanted him to end up with.

He already had a voicemail he was ignoring from his mother about the guy they'd made him go to dinner with last weekend. He was apparently looking for a date for some charity event. Dustin was damned if he was going to be someone's arm candy when he didn't even like the guy.

Leo, though? He could spend time around Leo and see what happened.

Nothing about this screamed fairytale romance, but it didn't stop him wanting to pursue the possibility anyway.

Just in case. You never know.

CHAPTER

Five

LEO

HE'D WALKED THROUGH BATTLEFIELDS AND FELT LESS NERVOUS. So why the hell was walking into the locker room making Leo's stomach drop?

The answer was easy: because he knew who else was there. Victor Frank, his best friend from childhood. They hadn't talked in five years—since he'd left Knoxville. It was easy to lose touch in a foreign country.

But now that he was back, and his shifts were more normal, they'd wound up on the same shift. It might work out well, Leo reasoned. He could sure use a friendly ear right about now.

"Hey. Victor?"

The man leaning against a locker and texting looked up, then lit up. "Holy shit. It *is* you!"

"Not many Leos around here," Leo laughed and strode up for a quick, manly hug.

"No shit!" Victor exclaimed. "Holy—are you all right, man? I thought you ran off and got shot. Jesus."

"Thanks for the positive thinking," Leo snorted. "How have you been?"

"I've been all right, yeah, man. Just been here, doing the city's work."

"Ah, jeez. Did you wind up heading to UT?"

"Nah. Man, who can afford that shit? Besides, they were giving all the good spots away to the *underprivileged students*," Victor snorted, his tone mocking. "You know, no scholarships anymore for plain old normal kids like us."

Leo blinked a few times as this sank in. He remembered Victor being kinda stupid about people who weren't from his very sheltered, middle-class, suburban world, but... not that badly. "What?"

"Yeah, man. So I ended up staying here. So I do a lot of traffic stops. Tickets. Fucking broke-ass losers begging me not to fine 'em. But what about you, man?" Victor punched his arm.

Leo's enthusiasm to talk to his oldest friend was rapidly waning. "Well, I was a pretty broke-ass loser," he said carefully. "So I enlisted. Photography."

"No shit! Like propaganda? That's so cool! Did you get to shoot the videos where they're like, running through the surf?" Victor made gunfire noises.

Leo jolted, his lip curling before he could hide his expression. "Yeah, a bit of it. A lot of documentary stuff." He kept it vague, not really wanting Victor to say anything about what he'd seen. He had the horrible feeling Victor's only experience of the military was glorified, stupid shooting games. "Got out, came here, learned forensic photography, and now I work here."

"No shit. That's awesome. Forensic photographer? All the horrible stuff?"

"Yep," Leo answered. He'd seen them enough, sure, but it didn't mean he *liked* it. "Not a lot of violent crime here. Lots of B&Es, that kind of stuff."

"Sweet, man. You liking it?" Victor laughed, his tone steel-edged.

Shit. He'd changed. Leo snorted. "Yeah, sure. Anyway, I better get going," he told him. "Thought I'd say hi since I'm back in town."

"We should hang out sometime. Cruise the chicks. Right? If you ain't tied down yet?" Even that was said with a jaded, ironic edge to Victor's voice.

"Sure, I'm free and easy. Thanks, man. See you."

Leo made his escape as quickly as he could and headed home, shaking his head as he strode for his car. At least he'd gotten that out of the way with, but clearly, things had changed with Victor.

Or had he always been like that? Was Leo the one who'd changed while he was away?

Leo sighed. No way could he talk to *that* guy and admit he was, like, the town's only virgin his age until two days ago, until fucking a guy and really liking it and having no idea what to do next.

He had real friends—friends who weren't assholes like Victor had apparently become—in the military. Some still serving, some who'd gotten out when he had or earlier. He could talk to them, but man, they wouldn't let him live this down.

No, I gotta work this one out on my own.

Leo turned to the best source for research on anything: Google.

Once he was home, he pulled out his laptop and typed in the query before he even thought it through: *how to be gay.*

It sounded dumb to his own mind, but he had to know. He had a fairly good idea how to date women from watching his friends and playing wingman for years. But men? What were the protocols?

There were different expectations, he was sure of that. He'd had a couple buddies in the military who swung that way. He knew there were procedures for everything from hitting on them in bars to, apparently, the order of sexual acts on Grindr dates.

Did he just text Dustin late at night one day and ask for a booty call? But he also wanted a friend—needed one. Whether he was ready to believe it or not, he thought he might need a friend way more than he needed the incredible sex. Which was a sad state of affairs.

Hell, romance didn't seem off the table. Dustin was sweet and interesting and nice. Leo had never seriously tried it before. No reason he couldn't try to woo him, right? Once he figured out how.

I gotta get out there and make new friends. Make a new life for myself.

Classes were a good place to start, and he had to leave now, or he was gonna be late for his today. Work, lunch, school, supper, sleep. That was his life lately.

Leo pushed himself to his feet and grabbed his bag from where he'd left it, already packed and sitting next to the door.

He had a Google search to get to. Maybe at the back of the class, while he tuned out another lecture on why their essays were unacceptable for the professional environment.

Sure enough, not even half an hour later, Leo found himself tucked in a corner at the back of the class, ignoring Professor Park. He was several weeks ahead of reading anyway, and the class was useless. The professor just read from the textbook. He'd heard better presentations in the mess hall.

Leo could kind of see the professor's point about useless reports, though. Everything he was finding about gay relationships was aimed at either older guys who were just coming out after marrying women or teens and even younger kids.

Nothing for the twenty-something who was stumbling into the obvious after a lifetime of managing to ignore it. Certainly nothing for guys his age who were already part of the workplace and weren't leaving notes in each other's lockers.

Unless…

Leo smiled, alt-tabbing to his word processing document and pretending to look attentive as Professor Park looked around the room to take notice of who was listening. He had an idea, and he could probably squeeze it in after class if he hurried.

It's gotta be worth a shot.

CHAPTER

Six

DUSTIN

Huh. That was strange.

Lying on the table among the mail he'd brought in today, Dustin spotted a folded note. Probably the neighbor complaining about his hedges or the state of his windows or some other weird little annoyance. Or, God, the HOA.

Just between us: treat yourself, gorgeous.

There was no signature. Enclosed was a $10 gift card for a local bakery—Dustin recognized the address as one of those cupcake places.

Dustin rolled his eyes. Which of his brothers was responsible for this? He was due to go out tonight with them. Normally they might have texted to make sure he was at home first, but any of them could have dropped by.

Speaking of which, *tonight* was actually *right about now.* Another evening getting caught up in sample analysis had meant he was home late from work as usual. He was often the last one to show up at the bar.

He grabbed a microwave meal, and showered and shaved while it heated up. Once it was choked down, almost scalding him, he grabbed his wallet and phone and keys again, racing back out of the house.

"About damn time you got here," a familiar voice bellowed across the bar, signaling to him where he should look for his best friends.

The whole group of them were gathered around the table.

Even Roman was here, now that his airline had just placed him on a short-haul route, and he was home more often. Deen, rock star and media darling, was taking a break from a tour, too. And Blane and Falcon were back from Paris.

"Whoa. It's actually all of us again," he grinned.

"Now that you're here, Mr. Tardy," Tyler snorted.

Dustin rolled his eyes back at Tyler and squeezed into the booth. It was getting awfully crowded with all these big guys, even as cozy as they all were with each other. There was barely room on the edge of the bench for him.

The extra boyfriends were the real problem: Roman was dating Oscar, Blane had Falcon, and Nico and Deen were a couple. Together with Tyler, Josh, and himself, there were a hell of a lot of them in a small space. Any more boyfriends and they were gonna have to add a table to the end of the booth.

At least there wasn't any risk of that for him. Not with his work hours.

"Glad you made it." That was Nico, giving him a warm smile. "Sounded like you needed the break."

"So, was it you?" Dustin accused Nico, giving him a suspicious look.

"Me what?"

Dustin wasn't fooled by the innocent look. "With the gift

card and note." But when he scanned the table, all he saw were blank stares in return.

Then Falcon leaned in, beaming at him. "Wait. Did you get a love note?"

"Oh, shit." Tyler rocked forward, too. "Tell us."

Dustin blinked and looked around. "No, seriously. If it's one of you guys…"

"Cross our hearts. Right?" They took a moment to look around at each other, and then all eyes were on him.

Dustin went red. He could feel it from the way his cheeks burned. Being the center of attention had never been his forte. "Oh. Uh. I got a gift card and a note saying to treat myself." He kept the *gorgeous* part to himself.

"An admirer!" Deen clapped with excitement.

Of course, his brain suggested several alternatives next: he had a stalker. He had a crazy ex. No, his one and only ex had been years ago, and he'd moved on to a bigger and better guy since. Some weirdo he'd hooked up with. Some weirdo he *hadn't* hooked up with.

Then the obvious presented itself: Leo.

He does seem sweet. He texted me thanks, and he held doors for me and stuff. And he knows where I live.

"Maybe?" Dustin finally allowed. "Or a stalker."

"Holy shit," Josh grinned. "Our little Dustin, all grown up. Let us know who to scare silly. It's been a while since that Bryce guy, huh?"

The boyfriends exchanged glances—Oscar, Falcon, and Deen hadn't been around back then.

But Dustin didn't need any reminder of his lacking love life. He sighed and glared, then glanced at them, feeling obligated to explain. "Bryce was my high school ex."

"His first sweetheart. Twerp," Blane muttered under his breath as Nico nodded.

"Whatever," Dustin dismissed him with a snort. In the end, they'd had to chase the guy off, but the details weren't important. It was a long time ago. At least he hadn't been abusive, just… not good enough for Dustin.

Of course, nobody had presented themselves as a candidate for his affection since, so he'd often second-guessed their choice, as much as he'd known it was right.

"He was just stringing Dustin along with romance to get sex," Josh summarized.

"Josh!" Tyler kicked him.

"Oh. Yeah. Sorry." Josh looked at him, but Dustin was more than used to a lack of sensitivity from the guys.

Dustin snorted. "Yeah, well. It was true."

"But he's not the be-all-and-end-all or whatever," Nico said with a frown, leaning forward.

"Yeah. Look at us. Chronic bachelors," Roman added, shaking his head at his new boyfriend, Oscar. "And we managed to settle down. If there's someone who wants to give it a go… *if* he's good enough for you…"

Dustin waved his hand. "It's not what I want, you know?"

At least, not something that was all romance to get sex. He could do no-strings-attached sex, or he could do romance, but none of this half-in, half-out bullshit. His reluctance totally had nothing to do with Bryce.

Dustin clamped down on the uncomfortable feeling and folded his arms. "I'll need more beer if you keep making those faces."

The skeptical expressions remained.

"Right. You don't want a boyfriend? We'll support that," Nico said slowly, "if that's what you really want."

"Good."

"But why don't you want to date him?" Nico continued. "Is he ugly? Rude? Stupid?" Each time, Dustin shook his head. "Bad fashion sense?"

Dustin laughed. "No. Jesus. I just don't think… I mean, we already hooked up once."

They just looked at him.

"And?" Blane finally prompted, as if that hadn't said it all.

Well, why the hell will he want the cow if he's got the milk? Dustin's family's words rang in his ears. They hadn't been aimed directly at him, but they sure as hell had been said very deliberately around him more than once.

Not only was he supposed to marry a guy for his money, but he was supposed to lure him along into marriage before he fucked him. Somehow. Like anyone did that anymore.

"My family wants me—"

"I know your parents have this boner for getting you hitched to some super-rich guy," Josh interrupted impatiently, "but *fuck that*. Man, you've been going on dates with every asshole they can find south of New York City and no dice. They don't own your dating life."

Dustin winced. "That reminds me, I have to visit them tomorrow."

Blane waved a hand. "So tell them to fuck off if they get nosy."

"But I…" Dustin trailed off, then sighed again. They were right. He was an adult, and he hardly kept in touch with his family anyway, except for their mandatory family lunches, which were invariably painful. His brothers had all come along at one time or another, and all of them agreed that they were "goddamn weird."

On the other hand, Dustin had no real reason not to go,

as long as work wasn't getting in the way. If the worst that came of it was being set up on a date with another boring lawyer with a gaudy BMW, he could handle that.

He'd already ruined the chance of a fairytale romance with Leo. What did he have to lose now?

"I don't know." That was Deen. "I think you should go for the guy who makes your heart sing. Even if you've already done a duet."

"Agree to disagree," Dustin said simply, which had always been his warning word to the others to shut up.

They settled down, reluctantly, and went on to discuss Deen's forthcoming single. That distracted Josh, at least, who had always been a lowkey fanboy. He'd since gotten Tyler to listen to Deen's entire discography. The pair of them looked like cats who'd gotten the cream as they listened in on the behind-the-scenes of production.

There is the question of why he left the gift card at all. I guess I'll have to talk to him to find out. The idea wasn't totally objectionable.

So that settled it... Dustin would call before he headed out to see his family tomorrow. And he'd stop by for cupcakes on the way back to reward himself for dealing with all of that.

Sounded like a plan.

CHAPTER
Seven

LEO

FUCKING TECHNOLOGY. THE COMPUTER KEYBOARD WAS LEO'S least favorite place to work. He much preferred being on location, framing shots and figuring out how to meter the exposure according to current weather conditions.

Actually getting back to the office, transferring his photos, and editing them was his least favorite job.

Leo sighed as he waited for his computer to process four images he'd taken with different exposures.

The program was automatically combining them so that all parts of the photo were visible—the knife lying in the shadows under the truck, but also the license plate and the driveway surrounding the crime scene, to show that they weren't hiding anything.

"Much rather be doing it in a darkroom," he muttered. His part of the office was a little quieter on weekends, but not by much. Crime didn't have a nine-to-five schedule, and he'd been called in on a Saturday to document the attempted vehicle theft at one in the morning.

The homeowner had scared the guy off, and he had no

doubt they were gonna get great prints off the knife, but they'd had to wait for him to document it before collecting it for processing.

Which brought his focus back to the person he'd been trying not to think about: Dustin. He wondered if Dustin was working that weekend or not. It was a small office, so it was just a quick walk around the corner to the forensics lab.

A little glance inside couldn't hurt.

After hauling himself out of his chair and stretching away the ache of lying on the concrete for many minutes in awkward positions, Leo headed over there.

"Knock knock," he said, poking his head around the doorway.

His heart sank. The lab tech on duty was Jared—a nice enough guy, but not Dustin.

Jared smiled. "What's up? Got anything for me?"

"Not yet. I'm combining exposures, but nothing exciting. They found the knife, but I think they dusted the truck handles for prints, too."

"Yeah, I've dealt with that already. Ran them for matches."

"Great. Sorry I couldn't liven up your day," Leo told him and jerked his chin in a quick goodbye before heading back to his computer.

The photo was finished, and it was exciting: clear as day. If he got called to the court to testify, he couldn't see anything that needed explanation. Knife, truck, empty drive-way. Easy as that.

His photos printed and job done, he clocked out, his mind already on the groceries he'd been about to buy. Thankfully he hadn't yet gone and bought milk, though come to think of it, the temperature in his car was probably similar to a fridge.

Leo sighed when his phone rang before he'd even left the

staff room. It wasn't his boss, though. He didn't recognize the number. "Hello?"

"Um, hi. Leo, right?"

The voice was familiar, but it took him a second. "Oh! Dustin. Hi."

"I got… I'm assuming it was your card. I really hope so."

Leo's heart soared. He'd almost forgotten about his errand yesterday. By the time he'd gotten to Dustin's place, there had been no answer. Scribbling a note on the notepad he luckily kept in his car for taking notes on short-notice calls, he'd at least been able to leave it for him to find.

"Right! Yeah. That was me. Did you treat yourself?"

Dustin laughed softly, and the sound was captivating. Musical. Uplifting.

Knock it off, Leo told himself. He had to reel the guy in slowly… assuming he even knew what to do with him.

"Yeah. I'm just glad it's not some random stalker."

Leo held his breath for a second. "Shit. I didn't sign it, did I?"

"No." Dustin's laugh was even richer this time, and Leo burst out laughing, too.

"Oh, man. Sorry. That was dumb. I'm glad you knew it was me, though." *Because that means you don't have other random admirers I don't know about.* "Um, and that you treated yourself. Good. I thought you deserved something nice." Leo cleared his throat, suddenly aware that he was walking through the office to the parking lot. His end of the conversation was very audible.

"Thanks," Dustin said. "It was… it was sweet of you. I thought it was my brothers, because nobody… I mean. I don't… I've never gotten random gifts." He laughed, sounding self-conscious.

Leo wanted to jump in and save him from it. "Me neither. But I think it's nice to be on the other end. Golden rule and all that."

"I must give great head." Dustin hummed thoughtfully.

Leo burst out laughing, his cheeks flushing. Thank God he was in the parking lot now, in case his downstairs brain decided to take that memory and run with it. And so that he could say this. "Uh, yeah. But I also wondered if you wanted to hang out again sometime. Like you said, friends or fun…"

"Friends *and* fun?" Dustin suggested.

"Yeah! Yeah, I'd like that." Leo felt the weight of pressure lift off his shoulders.

"Or are you talking a date?"

Boom. It was back, and Leo couldn't breathe for a moment. An actual date? God, what was wrong with him? He'd *had* dates before. This was no different.

Except that he'd gone on dates with women which had been incredibly awkward and hadn't led to anything more than a chaste kiss.

But he'd been balls-deep inside Dustin already, he'd kissed him and held him close and still wanted more. It was intoxicating and exhilarating and utterly new.

What if I act like an idiot and he figures out I'm like, the rookie on this team? Dustin had loved it when he took over. He wanted a man to be confident and in control and steady, surely. Not fumbling around trying to figure out how to circumvent his gag reflex at important moments.

"I'm talking a date." Fears be damned. Leo hadn't let them stop him before; he wasn't about to start now.

"Cool. I'd like that," Dustin said quickly. "When?"

"Does tonight work? I'm off-call this evening and onward," Leo told him. "Just in case."

"Tonight's good," Dustin agreed, then giggled quietly. "Right. In case of unforeseen events that extend into tomorrow, you mean."

"Yeah, those ones," Leo laughed. "The very unforeseen ones."

"Tonight at…?"

"I can pick you up at, uh, six?" Leo offered.

He could hear Dustin's smile in the way he enthused, "Great. Cool. Can't wait. Six. I'll be ready."

"I'll be there."

Leo hung up and struggled to unlock his car door. He was suddenly clumsy, his mind on everything he had to do before six o'clock: groceries, laundry, pick out a nice outfit, shower and shave, find his barely-used cologne, polish his shoes…

But his chest was warm with the kind of positive excitement and adrenaline he hadn't felt in so damn long.

Whatever the hell was going on, he liked it, and he wanted so much more.

CHAPTER
Eight
DUSTIN

THE AIR WAS CHILLY OUTSIDE, BUT DUSTIN HARDLY NOTICED IT as he paced back and forth in front of his house.

He'd never had a guy pick him up for a date before. Sure, he'd had guys pick him up for sex, but that was a whole different thing. Unless this was just sex.

Don't get your hopes up.

Hell, they could be going for a romantic drive and blowjobs. Men were like that. Dustin had gotten his heart broken once too often. He knew better, but he hoped anyway.

Totally worth lying to his family about meeting up with his brothers to get out of another painful family supper where he'd be interrogated about his dating life.

Avoiding those questions because he *had* a dating life was a whole new ballgame for him. He was used to avoiding them so that he didn't have to talk about his lack thereof.

A dark blue hatchback pulled up, and Leo leaned out of the driver's side and waved.

"You came," Dustin said breathlessly as he tumbled into

the passenger seat. It sounded much dumber—and needier—than he'd planned.

Leo just smiled at him. "I told you I would. Notice I resisted the immature joke there."

Dustin laughed. "I admire your self-control."

"It takes a great deal to be me." Leo's eyes sparkled with amusement as he waited for Dustin to buckle up, then drove.

"Where are we off to?" Dustin folded his hands in his lap, trying to subtly wipe his palms on his knees in the process.

"I thought a restaurant first, and we'll see how tired or full we are afterward," Leo offered, the end of the sentence rising in a question.

"Yeah. That sounds great."

Too late. Dustin's hopes were so far up that he was in danger of a commercial airliner collision. Or maybe a Space Station impact.

He's taking me to an actual restaurant.

"It's… honestly, it's been a while since I've gone on a normal date," Leo said with a sheepish chuckle, glancing sideways at him. He looked anxious about Dustin's reaction.

"Oh, that's fine. Me too. I was literally *just* thinking that." Dustin laughed, reaching over the center console to lay a hand on his date's knee. "I won't judge if you can't remember which fork to use."

"God, no. It's not *that* fancy a place," Leo pretended to be horrified. "I wouldn't subject you to that."

He was dressed nicely, though, in slacks and a collared shirt. He looked sort of like he'd just gotten off work but was going out for Friday drinks. Dustin had a pretty similar look going on himself, since about all he owned anymore were work clothes.

"You've been living here a couple months?" Dustin tried

to make conversation, letting go of Leo's knee before it became awkward. "But you grew up here?"

"Yep, I was here all through high school."

"Me too. I grew up here, went to school, stuck around..." Dustin shrugged. "Just never really left. I appreciate the city more now that I'm older, I think. I couldn't wait to get out as a kid, but once I found out everything Knoxville really has..."

Leo nodded. "I appreciate more now that I'm back, too. Do you mind me asking how old you are? Or is that off the table?"

"A lady never tells," Dustin gasped.

Leo flushed bright red and looked over at him hastily. "Sorry. I just asked because... same class at high school..."

Dustin laughed. "No, it's fine. But—wait, *did* you go to my school? You do look kind of familiar." He'd just assumed he'd seen him around, but if he'd been gone for years...

"I think so. Did you know George Lovett?"

"Oh, shit," Dustin laughed. "Who didn't?" The popular kid from the first day of high school, George was *the* guy to know if you wanted to be popular. Naturally, he hadn't, and his brothers hadn't, either. "Know *of* him, I mean."

"Yeah? I hung out with Victor's crowd, if you remember..."

Dustin made a face. They'd been assholes, largely. *This guy had hung out with them?*

Before he could say anything, though, Leo sighed. "Yeah, I know. I talked to Victor the other day. God. Was he always that much of an ass?"

"Uh..." Dustin couldn't say he'd kept in touch to find out how much worse Victor could have gotten, but he wasn't about to give a character reference to him based on high school. "He didn't actually shove anyone into lockers, but he sure as hell stood back and laughed."

"They didn't," Leo gasped, glancing over.

Dustin shook his head hastily. "Only a couple incidents here and there. I was buddies with a bunch of bigger guys—Nico, Roman, Blane, Josh, Ty."

"Shit. I know you," Leo exclaimed. "I mean, we never really talked, but the six of you were like a clique in the last couple years, weren't you?"

Dustin brightened up. "Yeah! Significant brothers."

"That rings a bell but…" Leo shook his head. "What's that from?"

The story never got old. Dustin recounted it in brief: the school dance where they were told they had to bring girls as significant others, and offered each other up as significant brothers.

"And it just stuck."

"Man. I know I heard something about that back then—" Leo started, then cleared his throat.

"And it was in the middle of a gay joke, wasn't it?" Dustin half-smiled. Nostalgia rarely took hold of him. All it took was remembering how things had really been back then in Tennessee—hell, still were in most places. "It's okay."

"I never really teased anyone, but… I guess I didn't notice what anyone else was doing. I was in my own little world," Leo admitted. "It took a long time before I learned to watch my surroundings. Through a lens. Darkly," he chuckled.

They were pulling into the parking lot of a nice Italian place. Traditional, safe choice—and romantic, Dustin couldn't help but notice.

"Okay. Ready?" Leo asked, like they were about to walk into a laser tag place.

Dustin laughed. "To tackle some serious spaghetti? You bet."

"Lady and the Tramp-style?"

"Oh, God." Dustin shook his head. "Kissing with spaghetti sauce? No."

"And I'm not sure I can watch you suck a limp noodle into your mouth without *my* noodle getting… less limp." Leo's cheeks were red as he laughed. "Okay, I think I undid my hard work avoiding the innuendo earlier. Sorry. I'll try to be appropriate in the public eye."

Dustin grinned at Leo and squeezed his knee again, then unbuckled. "Only in the public eye, though."

"Yes, sir," Leo teased.

As Dustin let Leo lead the way, he felt a hand settle in his lower back and his heart raced. Being shown around in public—shown off, even… But then it was gone as they approached the door, and Dustin bit back the disappointment. It was only sensible not to invite trouble.

"This way, please."

They got the fuss and rituals done with—the host looked slightly confused about whose chair he should pull out. He settled on Dustin, no doubt because he was the smaller one of the two.

Dustin exchanged looks with Leo, who looked like he was trying not to laugh.

"I get it a lot," Dustin said once they were alone with the menus and a candle between them. "The sweet, delicate one must be the girl, right?"

Leo shook his head. "I don't get it. Next time I'll insist I get served first since I clearly have more curves."

"If we're counting biceps, sure," Dustin snorted. "You're more graceful, though. I'll give you that."

"You're efficient," Leo countered. "The way you walk—you've got somewhere to be, and you don't let anything stop you."

"Are you watching me at work?" Dustin playfully accused Leo, who turned red again.

"Anyway, the menus! I checked them out online. They looked good." Leo buried his face in his.

Dustin had to choke back his laugh. It was all so early and new, but he felt like he was getting to know Leo. There were no pretenses with this man. So far, he was just *him*, as far as Dustin could tell. It was so refreshing.

Choosing food was the easy part.

The hard part came after they'd handed back the menus and had nowhere else to look but each other. Dustin could only kill a few seconds by looking around the place and commenting on how nice it looked.

"So, uh," Dustin said instead, steeling his nerves. *Just pretend you're friends. Get to know him.* It hadn't escaped his notice that of his coupled-up friends, many of them had started as friends, or at least hadn't intended to date seriously. Taking the pressure off had to help. "It took you a while to start noticing your surroundings, you said."

"Ah. Yeah," Leo nodded. "I'm a photographer—well, you know that part. I got hired here because of a buddy. Just got out of the military, doing the same kind of stuff, but with more glory."

"Oh, wow. Overseas?"

"Yep. All over—wherever they wanted me," Leo told him. He looked tired just saying it. "It's good to be home, in one place, just… putting down roots. You know?"

Dustin nodded. He'd never moved around like that, but he could imagine. "Why did you get into that?"

"Needed the money," Leo admitted easily. "There weren't a lot of other career options that interested me. I could make a living from photography. Back then I never would have considered forensic photography. Now, it doesn't seem like such a big deal."

Dustin nodded slowly. Suddenly Leo's steady mannerisms and maturity made sense. "Yeah, I see."

"How about you? How'd you end up in that sexy lab coat?"

Dustin found himself tongue-tied for a moment and had to take a quick gulp of ice water. Hearing himself casually called *sexy* was nothing new. But usually it was by a guy who was trying to persuade him into bed, and it felt manipulative. Which definitely had nothing to do with Bryce, whatever his friends had to say about it. But the way Leo said it? It just sounded like a casual comment, even a statement of fact. Like he wasn't trying to woo him, but calling things as he saw them.

"Um," Dustin finally answered, "I was always into science. I wanted to do something to help the country, and... well." If Leo was going to share, he might as well. "Honestly, I wish I'd been able to enlist, too. My family was pushing me to do it since I didn't know what I wanted to do except *help the world*, you know?"

"Uh huh." Leo watched him intently, like he was drinking in his words.

Dustin blushed again. It wasn't as hard as usual to be the center of attention when it was Leo's attention. "But can you imagine me getting through boot camp? And even then, what would I really *do*? They wanted me to either join the military or marry a rich guy. They didn't care it's a guy, just that he's rich, you know? But that's not me. I wanted to do something special-ized to help the world. So I thought: police, fire, ambulance, that kind of stuff. Which led me to thinking about forensics as a way of… solving crimes, helping people. Getting justice."

"That's really admirable," Leo said softly.

Dustin shook his head. "I don't do it for admiration. It's a need."

"Oh, I know. I feel like that," Leo answered, which blew Dustin away for a moment. "I got a little wrapped up in all that stuff I used to do. Won some awards. I don't love all of what I did now, but… I made a difference, too. I showed the truth. But I was starting to tell too much of the truth—I don't know if they would have wanted me back, and I didn't want to go back. I was thinking about being a documentary corre-spondent next, because I wanted to show how much all sides of any conflict—there are never just two—hurt. And then I realized I can do the same thing on a much smaller scale right here. Settling things fairly, showing the record for the courts. It's important stuff."

"Really important," Dustin murmured, still trying to process everything he'd heard. "I can't imagine. Wow. Good for you."

Leo shook his head. "Every piece of media has a narrative. Every photo, every song, every poem. Every TV show, even the stupid reality shows. All of it. They all have a story that someone wants you to believe. And I want to make sure the stories in the legal system are the truth. I don't want inno-cent people dragged into things. I don't want guilty people getting away. And I really don't want victims to suffer with-out… justice."

Then, as if coming to his senses, Leo looked embarrassed,

his cheeks red as he stared at the table. He mumbled, "Sorry. Not really first-date talk."

But Dustin was still breathless. There was something stirring deep in his chest. Leo's voice was raw and authentic and *true*. He hadn't had a guy talk to him like this in… well, ever. Even his ex-boyfriend had been telling stories he wanted him to believe. His eyes were hot and achy at how real the words felt to him. "That… No. No, don't apologize. That was beautiful."

Leo laughed quietly, glancing up at him. "Yeah?"

Dustin held his gaze, trying to convey that he was telling the truth. "Yes. That's… I like being able to talk honestly, you know?"

"Yeah. Yeah, it's not often I get to, either," Leo said slowly.

Thank God their meals came, giving them both space and a few minutes to sort out utensils and comment on the presentation. They didn't return to the conversation, but it still tinged the air between them. There was a rawness and trust there that left Dustin breathless.

As they dawdled over the last of their meals, utensils set aside, Leo brought up work again. "So, did you see the poster in the staff room for the cake auction?"

"Oh, yeah. That's tomorrow." There was a fund started for an officer with cancer, and Dustin had been meaning to contribute. "I was gonna bring something, but… I never got around to it."

"I was going to bring something, too," Leo said. "Wanna collaborate?"

That actually sounded fun. Dustin perked up and grinned. "Cool! Yeah. I'm not much of a decorator. Your eye must be better."

"I guess it's all right. I'm okay with color. Creating stuff from scratch has never been my strong suit, though," Leo admitted. "I was worried I'd make the ugliest cake out there."

Dustin laughed. "Me too!"

"And I don't have any good recipes," Leo added. "I have a cake pan, but I've never used since I moved in a couple months ago. I was gonna get a box."

"No, no. We'll do it from scratch," Dustin told him. "What, tonight?"

"It's tomorrow. Either tonight or tomorrow morning."

"It'll need time to cool off, right?" Dustin grinned. "Let's do this. We can do it. Two great minds, right?"

"I haven't tested my smoke detector in a while…" Leo grinned. "Can you attest to a spotless baking record?"

Dustin rolled his eyes. "Oh, come on. Have *some* confidence in us. I've never started any major fires. We're adults. We can figure out how to make one little cake."

When Leo grabbed the bill, Dustin tried to argue, but Leo waved it off. "Let me. Please."

Dustin's cheeks flushed. He looked down at his hands, twisting them together in his lap while Leo paid and made small talk with the waiter.

He's treating me again. I'm going to need to figure out something to do for him.

"Thank you," he said once they were on their way out of the restaurant.

"Of course. You're saving my bacon by making a decent cake. Then I don't have to avoid someone's gaze for years to come, knowing they had to taste my mushy concoction."

Dustin zipped his jacket up against the cold and winked, moving away from Leo to the passenger side of his car. "That's a new euphemism."

Leo burst out laughing. "You're more trouble than you look."

"And more than I'm worth, some say," Dustin joked.

"No," Leo immediately told him, pausing with his hand on the driver's door handle. "Not at all." He gazed at Dustin intently, like he was making sure he knew that.

Oh my God. I think he likes me.

Dustin just jerked his shoulders in a quick shrug and smiled. He fumbled to open the car door and get inside so he could open Google on his phone. Not only did it give him an excuse to cool down after the compliment, but it was a critical task. Everything rode on him finding a good cake recipe online, and he couldn't remember the last one he'd used.

He chose one with five stars and held his breath as he looked over the ingredients list and read it out for Leo to confirm he had everything they needed.

The internet couldn't be wrong, could it?

CHAPTER
Nine

DUSTIN

"I KNOW IT'S NOT A MANSION OR ANYTHING," LEO SAID AS HE let Dustin into the house, then gestured around. "But it's mine."

"No, it's nice," Dustin told him. Of course he wouldn't have said anything else, but it was true, too. "A bit bachelor, but we can fix that."

"Oh. Someone's thinking ahead," Leo teased.

It took Dustin a second to get it, and then he blushed and quickly looked back at him. "Oh, sorry. I mean… It's not… Ha. I meant—"

"I know," Leo laughed. But they both noticed that Dustin also hadn't come out and said that a relationship was off the table. By unspoken mutual agreement, they let the moment pass and Leo just gestured toward the kitchen. "After you."

"Ladies first?" Dustin returned the good-natured teasing, smirking when Leo blanched. "Why, thanks, good sir. Don't worry. I know I'm the token twink."

Leo snorted and shook his head. "Surrounded by all those great big guys in school, I can see why."

"It'd be easy to develop a complex. But…" Dustin shrugged. "Having them around had its benefits. Oooh. Nice kitchen."

"Thanks," Leo grinned. "So, have at it. What do we do?"

"You have to get the ingredients out, or I'll have to rummage through your drawers," Dustin winked.

Leo smirked back. "Oh, that's a bit old-fashioned."

"I can be," Dustin shrugged, avoiding Leo's gaze as he headed to the fridge to check for eggs and milk.

"In dating?" Leo asked after a few moments of silence. "Tonight was pretty traditional."

Dustin quickly looked over. "Thank you." He didn't want Leo to think he was ungrateful. "It was. It's been perfect. I just…" he trailed off.

"Hm?"

Well, he was about to stick his foot in his mouth. Dustin fiddled with the milk carton and box of eggs as he set them on the counter. "When we met at the bar…"

"Ah," Leo murmured. He seemed to know what was coming, but he didn't interrupt, just waited for Dustin to finish.

Come to think of it, even that was weird. He loved his brothers, but they could talk over him sometimes. Dustin had learned to be loudmouthed when he really wanted to be heard, but most of the time, he didn't bother.

"You kind of implied that you're straight," Dustin said. He didn't want to scare Leo off with this conversation, but he needed to know. "But you're basically being Prince Charming right now. I don't care what labels you use. I just wanna know… are you going to freak out later?"

Leo's gaze was perceptive, perhaps too much so. It was

hard to hold. When Leo answered, his voice was thoughtful. "It's not a problem so far. I don't think it will be. I don't tend to date much. I'm not, you know, stuck on myself being one thing in particular. I just thought… well, when I walked out of the bar, I knew my gut instinct was telling me to pursue this."

"That's pretty rare, you know." Dustin smiled. "Someone —especially a guy—who's willing to look past the story everyone tells about sexuality. But it makes sense, given what you said earlier."

They were leaning against the counter facing each other, their hands both on the countertop just a few inches apart.

The chemistry was easy to feel between them. Dustin's heart sped up. His hand itched to touch Leo's, like a circuit in an electric field that wanted to be completed. When he did, he heard the sharp intake of breath from Leo.

Then, Leo leaned in to kiss him. It was soft but lingered on his lips, gentle and tender and everything Dustin's kisses usually weren't. Leo was also the first to pull away, clearing his throat as he opened cupboards and noisily took out mixing bowls and spoons and a cake pan. "Right, this should be everything we need."

Dustin tried not to beam, but he failed. Hell, he could tell his cheeks were dimpling. He set his phone up on the counter to reference the recipe. "You preheat the oven, I'll start mixing."

"Aye aye."

They worked well together, making conversation about nothing important as they carefully followed the recipe. Sometimes they collided, but it was an excuse for a quick kiss or grope.

And it was so damn fun.

Dustin couldn't remember the last time he'd had a date like this—weirdly romantic, playful, full of joy and joking around.

"Oh, whoa! Dude," Dustin scolded, pushing Leo away from him when he tried to lean in for a celebratory kiss after they'd finished mixing the batter.

Leo looked wounded for a moment, and Dustin felt like he'd just kicked a puppy. *Those eyes could make me do dangerous things. If I'm not careful, I'm going to fall for him.* "What?"

"How did you get cake batter on yourself already?" They hadn't even poured it into the pans yet.

Leo glanced down at his t-shirt and then snorted with laughter. "Oh, I don't know. Special talent for messes."

"I remember some pretty contained messes last time," Dustin teased. "Go on, you pour it in the pan then. You're already elbow-deep in—it's all over your arms, too! How vigorously did you beat the batter?"

"You said vigorously," Leo said, sheepishly.

Dustin laughed. "Vigorously means for someone like me. Not with arms the size of yours."

Leo whipped his shirt off and adopted a romance novel cover pose. "Go on. Tell me more."

Dustin almost doubled over with laughter, though he couldn't help admiring that goddamn perfect body of his. "That's enough to make me swear off romance and head for the bedroom."

"If you're all romantic, though..." Leo started as he slid the cake into the oven, then nudged the door shut with his hip. "How are we going to pass the time until this cake is done?"

Dustin blinked at him, then laughed. "Hey, I didn't say I was *all* traditional. I did fuck you the first time we met at the bar. Well, that wasn't technically the first time we met, probably, but we can call it that."

"True," Leo smirked. "And I'm glad I met you now, when I'm observant enough to notice a good thing."

Dustin wasn't sure if he was blushing again or it was hot in the kitchen from having just opened the oven. He couldn't seem to contain himself around Leo: blushing, having trouble finding words, and… oh, no.

Crap. Too late. I already like him.

"Besides, this is real life," Dustin said to distract himself from his thoughts. "We take what we can get."

Leo set his oven mitts aside and walked toward Dustin. As Dustin leaned back against the counter, Leo pinned him there with a hand on either side of his body. He was watching him intently—not quite like a predator, because there was also a question there. He was making sure Dustin was okay with this. "You shouldn't settle for less."

Dustin nodded slightly. *Oh, if only you knew.* "That's why I don't date much."

"Good. I mean, not…" Little lines around Leo's eyes crinkled every time he got tongue-tied and tried to explain himself. It was adorable. "Not *good*, but—aw, hell. Good for me. Let's settle on that."

Dustin laughed. "Good for tonight, definitely." He leaned back against the counter, tipping his head up for a kiss.

Leo took the moment and pressed their bodies together, his hand sliding over the counter to grip Dustin's as their lips slid along one another's—slowly again, but it felt like something between them deepened every time.

Or maybe that was Dustin's wishful thinking.

"I want to treat you some more," Leo murmured. "I don't get the feeling many people do." Ouch. The sting must have shown on his face, because Leo winced and pressed another kiss to his lips. "Sorry. I didn't mean it that way."

"No," Dustin murmured, resting their foreheads together for a moment and closing his eyes. More intimacy than this was hard to handle yet. "You're right. I just don't know what to do in return. I hardly know you, but... but I'm already telling you things..."

"I know," Leo whispered when he couldn't figure out how to continue. "But I trusted you right away. There's something about your face. I just knew I could."

Dustin chuckled quietly. "There's something about your honesty from the first moment, too. I don't have to pretend."

"That seems like a solid foundation for a... for something." Leo changed his mind on whatever he was about to say, and Dustin was partly glad. He didn't want to put a label on anything and constrict it before it blossomed.

"But for tonight... I'm not such a traditional romantic that I don't want sex, too," Dustin continued, trying to keep his mind focused. He grinned. "It was good with you. A lot better than most Grindr dates."

Leo grinned. "I'm glad you said that, because I had some ideas."

"Ideas that can take up..." Dustin checked the timer. "Half an hour?"

"God, I hope so." Leo winked. Before Dustin could crack another joke, the other man was sinking to his knees in front of him and digging around in his pockets.

Dustin gasped and grabbed the edge of the counter as blood flushed through him. His knees buckled, but he caught himself. When was the last time he'd had a good blowjob? A few hookups came to mind, but the oral segment of each had been forgettable.

He was halfway to hard by the time Leo had fumbled the button and zipper of his pants open. "Oh, yeah. I'll forego all tradition in the name of *this*," he murmured, slowly letting go of the counter and resting a hand on Leo's broad shoulder.

Leo grinned up at him as he cradled the length in his hand, stroking slowly. He had a knack already—firm, but not painful. "That good?"

"Yeah. The head's the most sensitive, really," Dustin murmured. "You can drive me crazy with that."

Leo's eyes lit up. "I like that you communicate. Makes my job easier." He rolled the condom on, slowly but carefully, just like everything he was doing right now. The gentleness with which he held him was a sharp contrast to previous experiences.

"I wish more guys would." Dustin shook his head. "What is this *too cool to talk about what I want* bullshit? Doesn't make sense."

Leo laughed and then leaned in closer. He licked from the base to the tip of the shaft, almost experimentally, then started alternating strokes with licks around and along him. The wet skin felt strangely good in the cool air of the house.

Dustin pressed his fingertips into Leo's shoulder as he steadied himself against the counter with the other hand. "Ooooh! I like that."

"I like *this*, so we're even," Leo commented. He pressed a kiss near the head, just under it.

Dustin wasn't sure he'd ever had a guy giving him head talk back, but he kind of loved it. "But I'm gonna go nuts soon. I want you to suck me," he murmured.

"Hm?" Leo teased, shifting on his heels to look up at

Dustin as he let the flat of his tongue rub and wrap around the head, smoothing it across sensitive skin. "I'm not sure I heard that."

"Fuck," Dustin whispered, his nails digging in. "Oh, that's good too."

Leo kept it up for a minute, the wet warmth tantalizing but not yet enveloping him. He was so hard now, his heart pounding. Small gasps and moans escaped his throat, however he tried to hold them back. He was starting to suspect Leo was deliberately trying to draw them out of him.

Dustin was panting for breath by the time he moaned, "Please?"

The heat of Leo's mouth wrapped around his cock, and it was totally worth begging him for more. The suction closed in around Dustin as Leo wrapped his hand around the base of Dustin's cock, stroking as he focused his tongue on lapping and teasing the head.

"Fuck," Dustin moaned. "Fuck, fuck, fuck." He was so not holding out long under these conditions. Leo was paying attention to his moans, doing more of what he most liked, and not holding back enough.

Someone isn't used to making sure his man stays hard enough to fuck him afterward. Dustin spared a moment for amusement. The arousal was so damn hard to hold back. He rolled his head against the cabinet and pushed his hips forward.

Leo let him fuck his mouth, the head sliding over his pursed lips while his hand still squeezed the hard cock. And then Dustin opened his eyes for a peek at the hard shaft sliding in and out of that beautiful mouth and past it to Leo's own cock in his hand—when had that happened?

Leo was stroking himself hard and fast as he knelt there, sucking him off.

"Fuck," Dustin gasped, both hands going to Leo's shoulders now to grab tightly. "Oh my God. Baby, I'm almost... I'm..." His voice trailed off.

Leo let him slide out of his mouth and he gasped, about to growl in disappointment and need. But Leo was sliding the condom off his cock and tossing it aside. Then, he kept stroking Dustin in quick, practiced jerks of his wrist.

"Oh! Fuck. Are you sure?"

"Very." Leo leaned back, Dustin's cock inches away from his chin. His hazel eyes were open and on Dustin's, showing remarkable trust in his grip and Dustin's aim. "Come for me, baby. You're so close. I can feel it. You're so hot," he whispered, his fingers giving welcome friction against the length of Dustin's arousal.

It was the hottest thing Dustin had ever seen. Dustin gripped Leo's shoulders hard, to keep himself upright.

It was just a few more desperate thrusts of his hips into Leo's hand before he came. Jets of passion streaked Leo's cheek and chin and even his chest as Leo leaned back, stroking him through his bliss. He couldn't even think straight, and Leo's quiet moans of arousal and appreciation didn't help.

"So fucking hot," Dustin whispered, cupping Leo's cheek. He looked like he was just about there himself. Just as he thought that, Leo came, too.

The goddamn gorgeous man who had somehow picked him to spoil rotten was leaning back to aim his hard shaft at his own stomach. His hips jolted upward, and he moaned sharply as he added his own mess to Dustin's. "Fuck! That turned me on so much," he gasped as his hand slowed.

"I—I can tell," Dustin managed with a quick laugh. "Fuck.

Wow." He bent over to kiss Leo's forehead. "Hold on, I'll get you... uh..."

"I think a towel, by this point," Leo laughed.

Dustin couldn't stop staring at the sight. He was going to remember this for *years* of showers to come.

Unless they made even hotter memories in the meantime.

Dustin was suddenly pretty damn motivated to do whatever Leo wanted to keep him around. If hot sex would do it, he could have all the sex he wanted—romance or no.

He handed over paper towels and helped Leo clean up, pulling him to his feet so he could kiss him thoroughly in appreciation.

"All that and a couple minutes left to soothe my jaw before the cake comes out," Leo teased. "And, uh... I just realized. The cake will need to cool overnight before it's decorated, won't it?"

"You just now realized?" Dustin teased, grinning as Leo turned bright red. "You want me to head out tonight?"

"No! No, I—I was trying to say, if you want to stay..." Leo trailed off, then cleared his throat. "It's up to you. But we could decorate it tomorrow morning. We don't have to do anything else. I can stay on the couch."

"Oh, you," Dustin murmured, sliding his arms around Leo's waist. The feeling of Dustin's hands on bare skin was very distracting, but he tried his best to focus. "I don't want you on the couch. I don't mind staying with you."

"And a fun-filled weekend was had by all." Leo smirked. "We can head straight to the office party, unless you want to stop by home and change first."

"If cake decorations are spilled at the rate of cake-batter distribution, I'll need to."

As Leo laughed and pulled him in for a hug, Dustin pressed his face into Leo's shoulder to hide how wide his smile was.

This is the weirdest and best first date ever.

CHAPTER

Ten

LEO

"Um, if you want to borrow anything to sleep in, I have stuff. It's probably too big for you, though."

Leo was fussing over Dustin and he knew it, but he couldn't help himself. It had been so damn long since he'd had anyone in his house, and now… he didn't want Dustin to leave. Thank God he was staying the night.

He'd already offered again to sleep on the couch, but when Dustin turned him down again, he was glad. Now he was patting Dustin's pillow and testing the spring in it while he talked.

Dustin was giving him an expression he couldn't quite read—fond, maybe? He helped by interpreting it. "You're adorable. You might be the most adorable man I've ever met, and I know quite a few."

Leo hardly knew how to handle the compliment. He cleared his throat and waved a hand. "I'm just saying. Naked sleeping endangers balls."

"I'll take the risk," Dustin grinned, sitting on the edge of the bed to casually start stripping. "Better than *Local Man Found Drowned in Extra Fabric.*"

Leo burst out laughing. He was sitting on the other side of the bed in just his boxers, almost vibrating with anticipation. Not just at the show, either—at the whole prospect of this. It felt exciting and new and completely right.

He was glad Dustin liked him. He was even weirdly glad Dustin liked his house. It was a small place—a bungalow with two bedrooms, the second of which was being used as a study. Not that he was doing much studying there this semester, but it was nice to have an extra living room to hang out in.

And, more importantly, a kitchen with enough counter space to bake cakes and stand around drinking beers with his future friends and talking shit. The friends were also pending, but that would come in time.

It seemed modest to him compared to what most people had around here, but he wasn't really sure what was normal anymore. It was more space than he'd had to himself for years. Anything bigger than a closet felt like a mansion.

"Whatcha thinking?" Dustin quirked a brow.

Leo snorted. "I'm probably supposed to say something sexy about watching you strip, but I was wondering if you like my house."

"You..." Dustin stared at him and laughed. "Why?"

That was a good question. Leo answered on instinct, without really thinking through his words. "Because I want you to like everything possible about me. Is that... a little fast? It is, isn't it."

"I think it's normal." Dustin was naked now, distractingly, but *now* the conversation was on boring stuff and not sex. *Well done, dumbass.* Leo dragged his attention back to the conversation. He'd gotten enough action in the kitchen earlier, and he wasn't going to push his luck.

"How so?"

"Because people want to be liked." Dustin slid under the covers and Leo hastily followed. "Doesn't matter who we meet—a new boss, friends, a lover… we want to be liked."

Leo thought about it for a moment. "I guess so. I don't really have any friends yet. I was just thinking about that, too. It's nice to hang out with someone like a normal person again."

"It must be hard, uprooting yourself so much," Dustin frowned sympathetically. "I haven't really done it. I think I'm lucky that way. I used to wish that I traveled more, though…"

"The grass is always greener. There's my wisdom for the day," Leo smiled.

They were quiet for a moment, and the silence was more comfortable than before. The more time he spent around Dustin, the more Leo was fine with it. He didn't feel the need to chatter or make awkward jokes or anything.

"I guess we should get to sleep soon," Leo chuckled. "We have a long day with our coworkers tomorrow. Oh, man," he added under his breath. "The gossip."

"What gossip? We're buddies," Dustin said with a simple, bright smile. "They can fuck off."

Just buddies? Leo gave him a look, but Dustin wasn't clarifying, so he let it go for now.

As long as we're buddies who give blowjobs. He'd found that way hotter than he'd expected, and he hadn't even needed to try deep-throating this time. He'd been looking up tutorials online, but he'd forgotten to pick up popsicles today in his rush to get home in time for the date.

"You're thinking again."

"Sorry. I'll turn the light off and resume my thoughts," Leo grinned.

"Perfect," Dustin laughed, settling down against the pillow. "As long as you think your way to sleep."

"Sooner or later," Leo promised.

He'd heard about it from buddies who went and spent wild weekends with women they'd just met—mostly women, some men, but his gay friends kept it quieter. Flings, even. The idea of spending a whole weekend with this guy was thrilling.

Leo smiled to himself in the darkness as he settled down for sleep. "Good night."

"Good night," Dustin murmured.

Leo lay awake for a long time, listening to Dustin's breathing change to a slow, steady rhythm. Just when sleep finally came for him, he put a finger on the emotion that had been glowing in his chest like embers.

Trust.

He's changed everything, and he doesn't even realize it yet.

"Want some coffee?"

"I knew I liked you." Dustin smiled broadly as he buttoned up his shirt.

Leo thought he might explode with joy. He tried not to show it and turned to pull another mug out of the cabinet. "Okay, cool. Black? Cream? Sugar?"

"I like cream and sugar." Dustin pinched Leo's ass. He was flirting hard, and resisting was hard. Especially with the memory of yesterday: on his knees and watching Dustin leaning on the counter above him, his head rolling back in unrestrained pleasure.

Leo snickered. "Me too."

He hadn't expected his day to look so much brighter just because he started it off with Dustin at his side.

"So, do you mind dropping me off at home to change before we head in?" Dustin asked, leaning on the counter and gently poking the cooled cake on the counter.

"Of course. Wouldn't want tongues to wag," Leo teased. "Does that look ready to decorate?"

"Yep. Did you get icing sugar?"

"I did think that far ahead. It's in the cupboard to the left." Leo watched Dustin grabbing kitchen tools and stayed out of his way, supplying information when needed.

Leaving the decorating to him was a great choice. Dustin seemed to enjoy himself as he sliced the cake horizontally and assembled it. He was even humming under his breath.

"What are you planning?"

"You don't have food coloring, so just a simple checkerboard pattern," Dustin told him. "Chocolate and vanilla, since we made one pan of each."

"Oh, that'll look awesome!" Leo squeezed past Dustin to get to the breadbox. "Breakfast?"

"Yes, please."

It worked well—Dustin mixed up bowls of icing and started frosting the entire cake in white icing while Leo made them bagels, sausages, and scrambled eggs.

By the time they sat down for breakfast, Dustin had polished off two cups of coffee, but he was looking focused. Even as he ate, his gaze kept straying to the cake on the counter. The focus was absolutely fascinating.

"Just the tricky bit left, huh?" Leo prompted.

"Mmm." Dustin looked absentminded. "That's right."

Leo smiled to himself. He recognized that focus from work—his coworkers would often disappear into their own thoughts as they dusted for prints or analyzed samples. Seeing the same focus applied to a cake was kind of adorable.

"I'll take care of the dishes. You get back to the important stuff," he waved Dustin off after breakfast.

Good thing his kitchen was big enough for both of them to work, as long as he was careful. Dustin was utterly absorbed in getting all the lines on the checkerboard straight, and Leo was not going to be the one who bumped his elbow at the wrong moment.

"Done!"

The exclamation nearly made Leo, who'd been scrolling through the news on his phone, jump out of his skin. He glanced up from the kitchen island and then headed over for a closer look. "Oh, that looks cool!"

Dustin had managed to create a few little disks of icing and stack them up to resemble checkers, while others sat on the board.

"Holy shit," Leo revised his statement. "*Really* cool."

"You think?" Dustin glanced up at him, wiping his hands on a towel. "I'm not a pro or anything."

"No, man, that's awesome." Leo wrapped his arm around Dustin's shoulders and Dustin let him pull him in for a hug. "You're an amazing decorator. I had no idea. I'm gonna make you bake everything for me and take all the credit," he laughed.

Dustin snorted and hugged him back. "You can try. And you provided the kitchen. Mine's not really big enough for two. I don't even have flour. Oh, God. I hope the inside's good."

"If it's anything like you, I suspect so." Leo smiled.

Dustin didn't seem to mind the compliment. He flushed beet red and cleared his throat, then pulled away. "Right. We should get this ready for transport and then head to my place, right? Will we have time for anything else?"

"I doubt it. What time is the thing?"

"The thing?" Dustin laughed. "Two."

"The thing's at two," Leo mumbled to himself and nodded, glancing at the clock. "Yeah, that'll take about all our time, I think. Something made me sleep in today. Can't really remember what. It was sexy, though… and in my bed…"

Dustin winked at him. "Come on, then. Give me a hand with these toothpicks."

"I'll give you both hands."

"On the toothpicks, not my hips."

Leo pretended to pout and slid his hands away from Dustin's hips as he took the toothpicks from him instead. "Fine."

"For now," Dustin conceded, winking at him. "We'll see how late the party runs. Or how late we stay… which depends whether we get there on time."

Leo shivered with anticipation. "Toothpicks it is. Tell me what to do."

Finally, moving back to Knoxville felt like the right decision. Leo smiled broadly as he followed Dustin's directions. He was exactly where he was supposed to be.

CHAPTER
Eleven

DUSTIN

"Sixty bucks! That's more than I'd make offering my *services* to bar patrons."

Dustin choked on his nonalcoholic fruit punch and checked to see if any of his coworkers were listening to Leo. Nobody looked around, thankfully. "Don't sell yourself short. How do you know the going rate, anyway?"

Leo waggled his brows. "Wouldn't you like to know?"

As Dustin cracked up, he grew aware that his cheeks hurt. He hadn't smiled and laughed so much in a weekend. Leo had been his charismatic self all throughout the cake auction, and Dustin had drifted in his wake, enjoying listening in.

"Sixty bucks is pretty good, though," Dustin admitted once he'd calmed down again. "For a cake I decorated last-minute."

"The checkered thing was really good considering my lack of actual supplies," Leo praised.

"Yeah, I like how it came out." Dustin was still glowing from hearing everyone's comments on how cool the cake looked. He'd decorated a few birthday cakes for his brothers before, but only a few times a year and never with so much pressure or so few supplies. "I'm just glad it came out well, considering the cause."

"We don't get to taste it, though," Leo complained.

Dustin patted his arm, careful not to hold the touch for too long. "I can make another one for you."

Leo grinned. "Fuck yeah. I like this deal. I give you a kitchen, you use it."

"You give me a bedroom, I use it," Dustin added in an undertone with an innocent smile.

It was Leo's turn to blush and quickly look around. He didn't answer, just awkwardly smiled and headed for the drinks table.

Dustin took the hint. *No more flirting at work. Fair enough.*

It looked like the auction was wrapping up. They'd already bought—and shared with the other partygoers—a smaller cake each to fulfil their social obligations. Dustin had made small talk with coworkers he didn't really know and wasn't keen on socializing with until he was about ready to explode.

It was a burst of relief when Leo approached him again and asked, "Celebratory drinks?"

"To celebrate our very successful cake?" Dustin nodded, smiling broadly. "Yeah. Sure. Where?"

"At the bar where we met?"

Dustin laughed. "Are you sure?" *I'm never really sure what to make of him. Is he really just that comfortable with his new discovery?*

Leo winked. "Seems fitting. If you're up for it."

"Of course I am." Dustin followed Leo to the coat room and grabbed his jacket. "I think we've earned a little celebration."

Not that the weekend hadn't already been awesome. Holy fuck, had it ever. Fooling around with Leo in between baking, staying over at his place, and then going to a boring-ass work party and finding it suddenly much less boring than it should have been…

He hadn't wanted the weekend to end. Luckily for him, it looked like it wasn't over just yet.

"Hey, you bouncing early?" A guy Dustin vaguely recognized—they usually weren't on the same shift rotation—came up to Leo and slapped him on the back like they were old friends.

"Oh, hey, Victor. Yeah. We're just heading for a drink to celebrate putting our heads together to bake a successful cake." Leo jerked his thumb at Dustin, who instantly felt uncomfortable under Victor's gaze.

Right. Victor. From school. He recognized the same mean, narrow eyes, but it didn't look like Victor recognized him. In any case, Victor laughed at Leo. "Careful what you get yourself into."

"Oh, I can hold my own," Leo assured him.

"That's what I mean. Don't want anyone else doing it for you. Huh?" Victor grinned at Dustin.

Dustin smiled noncommittally like he had somewhere more important to be and headed for the coat room. Before he had his jacket on, Leo had joined him.

"Sorry about him," Leo muttered. "I didn't know he was… well."

"This bad? Yeah." Dustin resisted the urge to add, *You wouldn't.* Leo had been lucky enough to hide from that crowd —*in* that crowd—growing up. He was going to be in for a nasty shock as soon as he told the rest of the world about his sexuality.

If he even does, Dustin reminded himself. A lot of people didn't unless they had a long-term relationship, and they weren't there yet... if they ever got there. If Dustin even wanted them to.

That was a lot of *ifs* to think about, so Dustin put them aside and shrugged. "We heading out?"

"Yeah. Let's get out of here." Leo led the way, striding ahead to his car while Dustin tried to keep up.

It felt distinctly like Leo was running away from something, someone, or perhaps himself... but whether or not he knew it, Dustin wasn't sure.

"Heh, nice catch."

He was the third regular at the bar to congratulate Dustin with a high-five or shoulder slap... on his supposed new relationship or hot date.

With each one, Dustin tried his hardest to brush them off quickly and apologize to Leo, but so far, Leo had just looked amused and waved it off each time.

"I'm starting to think you're a lot more popular than you claim. Introvert, my ass," Leo commented in his ear.

Dustin wanted the floor to swallow him whole. As the guy grabbed his beer and headed back to the dance floor, he turned back to Leo. "No, but..."

"It's not a bad thing." Leo grinned and held up his palms as if showing Dustin he meant no harm.

Dustin still blushed furiously. He resisted the urge to press his own drink against his cheeks for a brief, welcome chill. "Yeah, well. I guess I'm here more than I think."

"Do you come here with, uh, the brothers you mentioned?"

"No, there's a dive around the corner. Well, that's not fair. It's not *that* bad. It's just… more…"

"Straight?" Leo teased, starting to grin again. "Less trendy?"

Dustin laughed. "Shut up. But yes." He clutched his beer like a lifeline, but it wasn't helping very much. "I come here after work sometimes. Especially when I stay late, and I've grabbed delivery or hit up some fast food on the way home. Not always to pick up guys, either. Just to hang out."

"It's like a living room," Leo said with an observant glance around. "For a different kind of family, a chosen one. No wonder they're happy for you—whatever assumptions they're making."

Dustin was stunned into silence for a moment before he nodded. "That's actually a good analogy." His embarrassment dwindled, replaced by gratitude. "You have a wise head."

"Oh? I'm usually told *big head*. I like that one more."

Dustin grinned. "It's in proportion to the rest of the shaft."

Leo burst out laughing. His laugh was always loud and unashamed, reminding Dustin of his other friends. He was shy sometimes—less so in their company—but they weren't. He liked that bold attitude.

"I like the idea of hanging out here, though," Leo said when he'd caught his breath. His hand found Dustin's, and their fingers tangled for a moment on the countertop. "It seems less lonely that way."

Dustin winced. The word hurt, but it was accurate. He didn't want to bring down the mood, though, so he just smiled. "I'm sure they wouldn't mind you hanging out here. Especially since you're more available than I thought."

Leo chuckled and glanced away, seemingly having his own moment not wanting to talk about it.

Dustin drained his beer and checked his watch. "Getting late for a Sunday night. I should probably head home."

"I was thinking the same." Leo chugged the rest of his bottle in a few gulps and set it down. "Let me call you an Uber."

"What a gentleman," Dustin teased to hide the moment of excitement. It was actually nice to be treated like this. But he couldn't take it as an indicator of anything more between them. Maybe Leo was like this to everyone... maybe he'd get bored... there were a hundred maybes that told him to be cautious.

They were soon standing outside the bar for the second time in chilly evening air, his shoulder pressing against Leo's as he watched the progress of the car on the app.

"This was a great weekend," Dustin murmured. "Thanks."

"No, thank *you*," Leo answered, his hand in the small of Dustin's back. "I learned a lot."

"Like how to decorate cakes? Or suck cocks?"

"Both," Leo snorted and grinned. He looked worried for a moment, and then the frown line between his brows disappeared. "As long as you had a good time."

"I did."

The car was pulling up, and Dustin's heart ached. *Is this it?* "So, I'll see you around at work." *Please don't ignore me there just because Victor might see us. I think my heart might break.* But it could go either way with a straight guy, or one who'd thought he was—he knew that very well.

Leo's expression was inscrutable. He let go of Dustin and clapped his shoulder, then tucked his hands in his pockets.

"Good night," he wished Dustin, and shut the car door. He was still smiling slightly as the car pulled away and Dustin looked after him.

If ever a man in business casual could look like the Mona Lisa—a tiny smile of nostalgia, but sad eyes—it was Leo right then. The sight was etched into Dustin's memory instantly, and then he was gone and the sidewalk blurred and he was heading home.

Alone again.

CHAPTER
Twelve

LEO

"Today is weird," Leo muttered. He resisted the urge to kick the office cubicle divider as he leaned back in his rolling chair.

The progress slider on his screen inched along. Goddamn department resources didn't allow for fast computers, which meant a lot of waiting around for image processing.

Getting back to work after his blissful weekend with Dustin had been strange. The weirdest work week Leo could remember, really. He was covering for someone flying out of state for a family funeral, too. The overtime money was good. He liked that part. But the job itself? He was starting to wonder.

Leo pushed through a few average tasks, meticulously creating the reports demanded of him while he waited for image processing.

At least he didn't have any court appearances. Not so much at first, but now that the gears of justice were grinding on and he'd been here a while, he'd been called to testify more. Which meant a suit and tie, and a waste of a day.

"Leo?"

It was Dustin, hanging back from the entrance to Leo's cubicle like he was afraid of getting too close.

Leo hadn't seen him since Sunday evening, and it was Wednesday now. He'd started to worry that he'd scared him off. "Oh. Hey, what's up?"

He fully expected a work question, but instead, Dustin stepped forward and awkwardly handed over a small box. "Something… for you."

Leo glanced around. Nobody around in earshot, so he smiled and glanced back at Dustin. "Yeah? Payback for the bakery treats?"

"Well, not that fancy. Just something… dumb little thing," Dustin mumbled and waved a hand, backing off already. "See you."

He was gone before Leo could call him back. Leo shook his head, watching Dustin power-walk back to the laboratory.

"What do we have here?" He tore open the plain wrapping on the box and lifted a layer of foam up. The back of a picture frame.

After he lifted the frame out and turned it around, Leo paused. He'd recognize that photo anywhere: Ansel Adams' photo of the face of Half Dome. It had launched his career into one of the bestselling and most famous photographers of all time.

Leo smiled to himself as he gazed at it for a few seconds, reminiscing about his photography classes all those years ago.

Then he put the frame on his desk and pursued Dustin to the laboratory, pausing when he got to the doorway and knocking on the open door.

"Hey." Dustin jumped to his feet from his computer and awkwardly smiled. "I wasn't sure if it would be your thing, since you don't do… landscapes… and whatever."

"No, I love it."

"I thought it could brighten up your house. Since it's such a bachelor pad right now." Dustin grinned at him.

"Oh." Leo grinned sheepishly. "I was thinking of putting it on my desk here at work, actually. A little inspiration. Since I'm here more than I'm at home."

"Oh?" Dustin leaned on the desk, which Leo took as an invitation to mirror his body language and lean on the filing cabinet next to him. "Why not?"

"College," Leo said simply, then remembered he might not have brought that up over the weekend. "Uh, I'm going back to school. VA's dime."

"Oh, cool… for a different career?"

"I don't know yet," Leo admitted. "Other than photography, I've never been able to see myself doing anything else." It was the kind of late hour in the office when the 9-to-5ers had left, and everything seemed a little surreal. Words came easier, and more freely. "I still can't."

Dustin nodded. He was sitting on his desk now, hands folded in his lap. "So why go back?"

"I don't know. I was hoping I'd stumble on something else I loved doing. But so far…" Leo trailed off, then sighed. "Sorry. I don't mean to dump my woes on you."

But Dustin just firmly shook his head. "I asked. I want to know. I mean, I did my forensics degree, and then I kind of… I don't know. Stumbled straight into this. But I feel like I'm here more than home, too. It's easier."

Leo blinked. "Easier to be at work?"

"At home, I just remember that I'm… well, I don't have

much of a life. My brothers are great, but they all have hobbies and stuff. I just do this." Dustin gestured around the lab.

"And it's important work," Leo told him. It was his turn to be firm. "We all rely on you. Couldn't get anything done without the forensics team."

"You're part of that," Dustin countered.

"I am. But I'm just documenting."

"So am I."

Leo scoffed and rolled his eyes. "If you're going to be stubborn like that…"

"I should have warned you, by the way: I can be stubborn." Dustin smiled cheekily at him. "Probably why I avoid being alone. I need someone to butt heads with. I always thought going back to classes would be interesting."

Leo nodded. "It can be, but it's very… well, freshman year. And all the kids are eighteen or nineteen or something. The professors talk down to you like you are, too. It feels like you're a league away from anyone else."

"Well, you can take evening classes in hobby-based stuff. Dancing, art, whatever," Dustin suggested.

Leo had had that thought before. "That doesn't lead to a career, though." He fidgeted with the drawer handle next to him.

"You looking to get out of this place?" Dustin gestured around. "How couldn't you love the bodies and blood?"

Leo laughed under his breath and tried not to let the old memories slip in. Dustin's sentence had opened the cracks he sometimes forgot still existed in that wall in his mind.

Dustin seemed to sense it, because he moved closer—a little too close to be strictly appropriate at work. "We all have those things that haunt us. Getting out of here before you break down about it is smart."

"I'm fine," Leo scoffed. "I've gone through all the treatment options. I'm not having flashbacks or nightmares or anything. I just don't like to think about it."

"Just making sure," Dustin murmured. His hand slid into Leo's, fingers filling the gaps between Leo's. "I've seen it a lot."

Leo squeezed lightly. "Me too. That's not the main reason I want to get out. I'm just… done with all of this. I feel like I've done my time. I need something that will make me feel more connected with people, not more distant."

Whoa. He'd never said that out loud, or even thought it to himself. Something was making him spill his guts to this guy he barely knew—a guy he'd spent one weekend with.

He trusted Dustin. He *wanted* him.

Shit. It had to be his dick talking. That was what had been broken or missing all along—incomplete, maybe. That was a good word. He'd defaulted to his attraction to women and it had totally blinded him to anything else he might experience alongside that, like… men.

Now he was overcompensating for all the attractions he'd missed out on.

It was a good, sensible explanation for the sparks between them as they held hands, Leo's body sheltering them from view of the door. But it didn't explain why he trusted Dustin as much as many of his buddies he'd spent months or years of intense action with.

"It's big of you to admit that," Dustin told him. "I won't say a word, of course. If you wanna stay on here or leave, that's your call."

"You have a good spirit," Leo finally settled on. He

squeezed Dustin's hand, tracing his other hand along the veins on the back of his hand, then over his knuckles. "Thanks."

Dustin winked. "Thanks, yourself."

Work, Leo reminded himself. That image was definitely done processing now, and this was the wrong place and time to hit on him. Why did he have to be a goddamn coworker, anyway? Why couldn't he have run into literally any other guy in that bar that night?

But they're not him.

Leo smiled and let go of Dustin's hand, then gave him a quick wave. He strode back for his cubicle, trying not to feel like he was mirroring Dustin's actions earlier and running away from him.

This was something he wanted to treasure—a real friendship, where he could share what bothered him before he even figured out what that was. It was utterly new, but the idea of losing it was already scary.

And that feeling could only grow stronger, right? That had been his experience up until now, anyway. No reason for it to be different because it was another man.

Leo shook his head as he fired up the printer. He was still distracted by thoughts of Dustin at work just a minute's walk away, wondering how late Dustin would stay and what Dustin's plans were for after work.

This was a thing. A crush, probably. A feeling he hadn't expected, and one that was sure as fuck inconvenient for coworkers.

I have to figure out who I am, and how I deal with this... pronto.

CHAPTER
Thirteen

DUSTIN

DUSTIN HELD OUT UNTIL THURSDAY BEFORE HE TEXTED LEO.

And really, after that sex, who the hell could have expected him to last any longer? It had already been nearly a week. Dustin pushed back against the gut instinct warning him not to get too close to anyone who hadn't offered any guarantees yet.

He didn't need reassurance from Leo. He just wanted more of whatever he could get from him.

Not seeing Leo at work that week was probably a good thing. Their work hours didn't happen to overlap, which stopped him from doing anything dumb like hanging out at Leo's desk all the time.

Dustin composed and deleted several versions of the text before finally letting himself press Send on a simple message:

Movie date tomorrow?

That would be Friday night, which surely made it kind of romantic by default. But just in case it wasn't clear, using the word "date" ought to help.

It was up to Leo to choose if he meant Netflix and chill,

or an actual movie out at a real theater. That would dictate whether it was just sex or something... more exciting. It seemed like an incredibly clever message, but it didn't relieve any of his anxiety while he waited for an answer.

Dustin didn't have to wait long. A couple minutes after he'd put down his phone and sworn not to check it again until he got an alert, it chimed.

It was in his hand before he consciously remembered reaching for it.

Sure! You choose. I don't know what's playing, haha.

"Oh my God," Dustin breathed out as he stirred the pasta that was that night's dinner one-handed. He fumbled to unlock and answer the phone with his other thumb. "He wants meeee."

Rom com? he suggested, his eyes on the screen more than the pot now.

Leo answered faster this time. *Appropriate for us, yes :)*

Dustin burst out laughing, his cheeks flushing. Well, that answered some of his questions. *IDK, nothing too slapstick has happened yet.*

Don't jinx us! Now I'll blame you when I trip into your arms.

Dustin grinned. *I'll catch you ;)*

I hope so ;) What time?

Dustin looked up movie times, poking in annoyance at the pasta. Why did it have to be almost done now? He quickly shot back a movie time and drained the pasta.

Leo had responded by then. *Sounds perfect. Can't wait!*

With that arranged, Dustin dumped pasta sauce into his slightly-mushy meal. Even the state of the pasta couldn't depress him, though, considering what he'd just gotten from Leo.

An actual date. Something that meant he wasn't cutting

ties and backing off now that they'd gotten close a couple times.

Maybe this had a future after all.

A Friday had never gone slower, but it was eventually almost time for Leo to pick him up. Dustin kind of liked this routine, too—standing on the curb with his hands tucked firmly into his pockets, waiting for Leo to pull up.

Leo was exactly on time again. Before his car had even come to a stop, Dustin trotted up to the passenger side. "Hi!" He swung into the car and buckled up.

"You're ready," Leo laughed. He hesitated, then leaned in across the console slightly.

Dustin smiled. It was clearly an invitation, so he met him halfway and pecked his lips. *Oh my God.* "Hi," he repeated, then realized he'd repeated himself. "Uh. Sorry. I am. How are you?"

"It's been a good week. Caught up and got ahead on homework. Lots of on-call stuff, though. And a couple court appearances. Glad to be off this weekend," Leo said. "You?"

Dustin waved a hand, hardly able to remember his work week now that Leo was around. He seemed to forget almost completely about that certain intoxicating *something* between them until he was back in Leo's presence again. Then, it was a fight to keep his hands off him. "Oh, all right. Nothing out of the ordinary."

The nervous tension between them was impossible to miss. There was a certain something different in the way Leo was holding himself, and Dustin squeezed his folded hands between his knees to stop them from shaking.

"Are you all right?" Leo was, as usual, much too perceptive. He was supposed to be driving, for God's sake. Keeping his eyes on the road.

Dustin slid his hands under his thighs instead and nodded. "Just chilly hands."

"Mmm." Leo glanced sideways at him again but didn't pursue it. Instead, he lightly smiled. "You found something lighthearted that we don't have to pay attention to?"

"Yes." Dustin dragged out the syllable for an extra second.

Leo winked. "Oh, no reason," he answered the unanswered question. "Except necking in the back row like high schoolers. I assumed that was what you had in mind."

Dustin's cheeks flushed and he giggled, his nerves settling down despite himself. *I can't be tense around him. It's so weird.*

"There's that smile I like to see."

Dustin could feel his blush deepening. Like a goddamn high schooler... except this time, he was doing it right. Not chasing the guys who were too full of themselves to pay him more than three seconds' attention.

Not that he was thinking about that right now.

He managed to make awkward conversation until they reached the theater and parked, but then there was no avoiding it: walking by Leo's side, figuring out how close to stick to him, whether or not to hold hands... It was a whole new world for him.

Leo seemed cool, relaxed, and unaware of all the internal battles Dustin was fighting. He stayed just a little closer than a couple of guy friends would, but didn't reach for Dustin's hand.

Dustin took the cue not to try. *It would be nice, though,* he thought wistfully.

"Two adults, please," Dustin heard Leo say. "And, uh, the date special."

The girl behind the counter giggled but punched it into the computer. "That's one popcorn," she said pointedly. "And two drinks."

Leo smiled back. "That'll be fine."

Realizing that Leo intended to pay, Dustin fumbled for his wallet. "Oh, I can—"

"No, no." Leo brushed his hand away from his pocket. "It's my turn."

Dustin was fairly sure Leo was taking liberties with the truth, but he wasn't about to insist and make things awkward. "If you're sure. Thank you."

"Of course. My pleasure."

"Screen three is through that way," the teenager told them once she'd given them their one enormous bag of popcorn and two drinks.

Dustin had to fight not to smile. He sure as hell didn't see any friends sharing popcorn. It felt more and more like a real date.

"I've been here... a couple times, I think? They definitely got refurbished since then," Leo said, carrying the drinks while Dustin balanced the popcorn and tickets.

"I came here once in high school," Dustin murmured. "On a date. We didn't get the date special, though." His cheeks flushed with embarrassment at the memory.

"How unromantic. This is much better," Leo declared. "Anything he did, I can do better."

Dustin laughed sharply. "Yeah. No doubt."

They were almost alone in the theater as they settled down and balanced the bag between them.

"What happened? Did you have to kiss a frog?" Leo asked.

"You can tell me to fuck off," he added, grabbing a handful of popcorn and stuffing it in his mouth. "Mm. S'good popcorn here though."

Dustin took a more dignified handful to munch on, one or two at a time. "Just some guy in high school. I wasn't gonna say. I never actually told my brothers. They only knew about my one ex, not this guy."

"Ooh." Leo sat up straight and gulped his drink, then turned to him. "Intriguing."

Dustin snorted. "Not because we had a fling or anything. The opposite. He was, I guess..." He searched to find a phrase that wasn't *leading me on* or *a closeted asshole*. "Not... what I needed."

Leo raised a brow.

"Fine. Closeted, and so not into me, either." Dustin winced at the memory, his cheeks flushed with embarrassment. Why couldn't he have just said he hadn't been here in a while and left it at that? "I tried to hold hands during a romantic bit of the movie and he laughed at me. He got me to, uh, play with him a little. That was about it. Didn't even get a kiss goodnight."

"What the fuck?" Leo was scowling now. "Asshole."

"It was a decade ago. My brothers and I were, like, the only out gay guys at school. Well, us and band club."

Leo snorted in amusement. "True. But that doesn't mean you're... I don't know. Target practice." He slid his arm along the seats behind Dustin's shoulders. "I'm sorry. There's a lot of shit I missed out on, apparently."

"Be glad you did." Dustin reached for more popcorn at the same time Leo did, and Leo took his hand for a moment.

"I am. But I'm still sorry you had to go through it." Then, Leo let go and gestured for him to take popcorn first.

Dustin fumbled to do so and get his hand out of the way, his heart racing. Leo seemed so… sweet and sincere when he said these things. He looked square into Dustin's eyes and told the truth.

That wasn't what Dustin was used to, at all.

"Um." Dustin finally found his voice, his heart racing as Leo's hand settled on his shoulder. "Thanks. I mean, I'm over it. Mostly. I guess. All that stuff from back then."

But when he thought about it, and admitted it to himself, he could trace back his cautious attitude toward dating to high school—Bryce, this guy and the rest of the bullies.

As if reading his mind, Leo hummed. "Are you? I don't think any of us really get over the things that leave an imprint." Leo's brows were furrowed now.

The ads at the beginning of the movie were playing, but the lights were still on, so Dustin didn't feel bad taking the chance to talk. "Like what?"

"Well…" Leo hedged for a minute, then caved. "My dad died before I even remember him. Mom remarried, and my step-dad was a little… hard on me, I guess. Just normal dad stuff. Didn't want me to go into girly photography stuff. Thought I should be a real military man and, I don't know, kung-fu my way through the jungle." Though his tone was light, his brows were still pinched in a way that made Dustin want to reach out and smooth the frown off his face.

"Shit. Sorry," Dustin murmured. "See, I feel lucky because *I* didn't get *that*. We all have our own… crosses to bear, or whatever."

Leo hesitated, then nodded. "I guess. It just felt like the normal stuff to me. You know, toughening me up."

"Which can be pretty fucked up," Dustin said and shook his head. "How are they about it now?"

"I don't talk to them about much." Leo sipped his drink and looked away, staring into the distance through the candy bar ad that was playing. "Just holidays, really."

"They live here?"

"Yeah. Yeah… do yours?" It looked like it took effort for Leo to look back at Dustin.

Dustin was happy to change the subject for him. "Yeah. I talk to them a little more than I'd like."

"Right, right. You mentioned that." Leo half-smiled. "The ones who want you to marry some rich man."

Dustin snorted. "Yeah, those ones. It's a weird kind of liberalism, you know?"

"Not bad, though?" Leo asked.

"I can't complain." Dustin shook his head.

The lights started to dim, and he breathed a sigh of relief. They'd survived a tricky conversation, and now they had a few hours of silence.

But hours wouldn't be long enough to forget all those strangely vulnerable things that had slipped into the air between them.

Fourteen

LEO

"HERE YOU ARE."

Leo couldn't deny it: he was hoping to be invited in. But, like a gentleman, he was dropping Dustin off at his apartment and giving him the choice whether to extend the invitation or not.

He hadn't been able to stop thinking about what Dustin had said—or hadn't said—before the movie began. It sounded like he'd gotten his heart broken, or at least wounded, and had poured himself into his work.

Not too dissimilar from Leo himself, then. Maybe not in romance, but he'd used work to escape his family and this town and his own uncertainty about the future.

He was no more certain what the future held now, but he knew himself a little better. Most of all, he knew his own courage and capability. So why was this one relationship throwing everything out of balance?

I know how to date. Just not how to date men. And there shouldn't be anything different, really.

Dustin was gazing at him, his expression tentative.

"Can I come in, or would you rather get some sleep?" Leo winked.

That seemed to be the opening Dustin was looking for. He relaxed and grinned. "I'd like you to come in. Who needs sleep?"

"Sleep is for the dead," Leo agreed, then sobered up as he heard his own words. More than anyone else, in their line of work, they both understood how short life was. Why not grab what was good with both hands and never let go? "And I want you."

Dustin slid out of the car and gestured with his fingers in a *come here* motion.

Leo shut off the car and locked it, following Dustin to his front step. They slipped inside the little bungalow together without saying a word until the door was closed.

"My room," Dustin murmured. "Now."

Leo slid his hands around Dustin's hips and pulled him in for a long, slow kiss. He took his time, letting their lips press together with the warmth that burned deep in his chest. His hand slid slowly up Dustin's hip and side to his chest, then up to his cheek to cup it.

Stubble burned his palm and pricked the tip of his thumb as he caressed Dustin's jaw, his other hand still wrapped firmly around Dustin's waist. Dustin swayed into him, his arms looped around Leo's neck as the weight of his slender frame leaned against him.

Leo easily supported him, letting his hand slide around to the back of Dustin's neck as their lips finally slid apart just enough for them both to catch a breath or two.

"What was I saying?" Dustin murmured.

Leo cracked a quiet laugh. "Did something interrupt your thoughts?"

When Dustin shifted his hips, Leo could feel the semi-hard length pressing into his thigh. He smirked. "Yeah, it did."

"Oh, hello," Leo greeted teasingly. His hand ran down Dustin's back to cup his ass and squeeze. "You were talking about your bedroom, I recall."

"Was I? Somehow we never get around to conversation when we're alone together." Dustin shook his head.

Leo winked and rubbed Dustin's ass, teasingly hooking a finger under his waistband and then sliding his hand down bare skin to cup the cheeks. "Would you rather discuss the news? Sports? Weather?"

With each question, Dustin shook his head and rolled his eyes. "Ugh," Dustin interrupted. "You're sure of yourself."

That couldn't be further from the truth, but if Leo was fooling Dustin, at least he was doing his job. "I don't think you mind that," Leo pointed out and grinned.

"It's hot," Dustin admitted in a simple, breathy whisper that turned Leo on.

Keep it up, Leo thought. He felt himself puffing up like a peacock. "Yeah? You know what else is hot?"

"Hm?"

"You, when you talk to me without… all that bluster and stuff I'm used to from my buddies. You just talk to me honestly, and that's… nice." Leo's words failed him at the very end and he grimaced. "Not nice. You know."

"Meaningful," Dustin suggested, his lips twitching into a smile.

"Yeah. Trusting. You trust me. And I… fuck, I do, too."

"I hope you trust yourself. You seem like a stand-up kind of guy," Dustin grinned. "I'd say you should."

"Oh, fuck off," Leo laughed. "I trust *you*, and you know it."

He turned Dustin around gently to steer him to the bedroom.

Dustin's smile faded, but his expression was warm as he glanced over his shoulder to Leo. "I do, yeah."

Leo shut the bedroom door behind them, and then Dustin took his hand to lead him to the bed to sit down. "Even after your experiences with that guy?"

"Which one?" Dustin's brows furrowed, and then his expression cleared with understanding. "Oh. The one I mentioned earlier. He wasn't a big deal. I only flirted with him for a little while. Then I realized..." he trailed off and grimaced. "I shouldn't have brought him up on a date."

Leo shook his head and scooted back on the bed until his head rested on pillows. He pulled Dustin against him. "Tell me. I want to know more about you."

Dustin hesitated, but he finally took his time and made himself comfortable in the crook of Leo's arm, his hand running across Leo's stomach in slow, distracting circles. "It wasn't that he was closeted, exactly. He never came out afterward, last I checked. I think it was some bullying crap. Trying to get my hopes up and dash them."

Leo hadn't paid that much attention to bullying tactics at school, so it took him a second to wrap his mind around it. "Really?"

"Yeah. There was him, and there was one of his buddies who asked me out to some dance in senior year—I never told my brothers about that, either," Dustin hastily added, presumably in case they ever met and the subject came up. *As it clearly so often does. He looks like he's never told anyone this.*

Leo gently stroked Dustin's hair and cupped the back of his neck, then kissed him. "And?"

"And," Dustin mumbled and shrugged. "I said *why*? And

he kind of fled. I think he expected me to be so happy for any attention that I'd, you know, fall over myself."

Come to think of it, Leo *had* known guys who did that to girls in school for that reason. He just hadn't paid enough attention to the extra level of homophobia. Hell, Victor had done it to the girls he thought were ugly and laughed about it. Leo had only gotten him to stop doing it by telling him it made *him* look desperate. He winced and shook his head. "Yeah, I see how that works. Was that what's held you back from dating?"

"No. There was my ex, Bryce, who was pretty much just… using me for sex. When my brothers figured it out, they scared him off." Dustin smiled, his hand running up under Leo's shirt. The way his fingers played against Leo's ribs was very distracting, and it took great effort to actually listen to his words. "I'm not used to having hot guys actually mean it."

Leo felt himself blush before he could stop. *He thinks I'm hot.* He tried to subtly flex his abs while Dustin touched him. "Yeah?"

Dustin's giggle was lighthearted. Leo was so busted. "Yeah, Hotty McAbs. Don't think I don't notice."

Distracting Dustin from the past—and the feelings that brought up—was Leo's goal, so hearing him laugh told him he was doing well, even if he embarrassed himself in the process. "Good. You should. I work enough on these. I'm going to show them off."

"Believe me, I've noticed." Dustin scooted up the bed to kiss him once, harder. Then, he swung a knee over his hip and pulled Leo's shirt up and off, straddling him and gazing up and down. "There. That's better."

Leo let him get a good eyeful, his grin bashful. "It's been a while since anyone has," he admitted.

"Good for me," Dustin hummed, winking. He leaned down to press slow kisses along the side of Leo's neck to his chest.

Holy fuck. Leo hadn't realized how many sensitive nerves were just waiting for the right warm lips and tongue flicks. Dustin was waking nerves throughout his own body with each slow, measured, light kiss.

"You tease," Leo whispered.

Dustin grinned. "Just taking my time. Enjoying myself." His nimble fingers slid slowly around Leo's nipple and then plucked gently, sending a sting of pleasurable pain ricocheting through Leo's body.

"Oof! Fuck," Leo moaned. He caressed Dustin's hair with one hand, his other resting on Dustin's shoulder.

"I remember how much you liked sucking me off in the kitchen," Dustin murmured, his warm breath teasing the nipple before he leaned in and sucked.

Leo's grunting gasp was enough of an answer. He tried to press his hips upward for contact with Dustin's thigh, but Dustin wasn't letting him grind yet. He moaned in protest and settled flat on the bed again, his toes curling into the bed.

He would let this sexy little twink torture him all night long if he wanted. It might drive him out of his mind, but the pleasure was far more intense than he'd expected.

"Good?" Dustin whispered. He ran his tongue around Leo's nipple once, then looked up.

"Please!" was all Leo could manage in response. "For fuck's sake. God, you're good."

The sight of Dustin's tongue peeking out between his lips as he dragged the warm tip up Leo's chest toward his nipple made Leo catch his breath in anticipation.

Then he was sucking it into his mouth, flicking the sensitive nub back and forth until Leo arched off the bed again, gasping Dustin's name like a prayer for more.

Dustin kissed his way over to the other nipple and Leo dug his nails into his shoulders, growling under his breath with how hard it was to resist flipping him over and ravishing him.

The pent-up tension shivering through him seemed to make his cock even harder. No amount of adjusting himself was going to help now. He needed to be naked now.

Dustin grinned, finally kneeling upright and shrugging his shirt off. "It's nice to be in charge sometimes," he commented while Leo's gaze hungrily wandered up and down Dustin's slender body.

"I like it, too," Leo approved. "I'm not used to... well. Being on the bottom." Then, his cheeks flushed. *Maybe he'll think I mean, like, bottoming.*

Dustin did indeed take it that way. He tilted his head. "Really? Never?"

Stay honest, Leo told himself. He gulped and then nodded slightly. "Do you usually? It just kind of happened last time."

"Yeah. I'm greedy." Dustin grinned, running his finger down the center of Leo's chest to pop his fly button open and unzip him. "But if you wanted to take a turn..."

"What does it feel like?"

Dustin winked. "No way to describe it better than feeling it yourself."

Leo's heart started to race. "Would you really top?"

"Um... hell, yeah," Dustin said with another big grin. "Watching you squirm around like that is hot as fuck."

I bet those assholes didn't let him top. Leo made his mind up. He wasn't ashamed of wanting to feel every kind of pleasure he could. Dustin had already shown him so many new things, and he wanted it all. "Then… yeah."

"I'll take it slow," Dustin promised as he pulled the rest of Leo's clothes off. He wasn't wasting a moment. "I want you to… to feel as good as you make me feel."

How could Leo not beam at that? His hard cock rested along his stomach now as he kicked the last of his clothes off, with Dustin's help.

Dustin squirmed out of his own skinny jeans and briefs and tossed them aside, and then he crawled back over Leo.

So much warm, bare skin slid together in one sensual movement that Leo's whole body shivered with pleasure. "Fuck," Leo whispered. Watching Dustin over him, moving with all the confidence and grace of a panther who had his next target in mind…

I want him. I want this. So bad I can't even describe it.

This ran so much deeper than any physical attraction he'd felt before. Leo had a hundred ideas for what he wanted to do to Dustin, and vice versa. He wanted *him*, not just *wanted* him. It was the subtlest difference, but now that he'd noticed, he couldn't forget it.

"If you wanna go get tested with me sometime, we could ditch the condoms." Dustin said it casually as he grabbed lube and a condom from the bedside table, but there was something too casual about that tone.

Leo caught his breath. Was that an offer of… monogamy? A relationship? Exclusive-friends-with-benefits? "You're not seeing anyone else?"

"Because I have so much free time for boring losers who don't even give me a turn to come," Dustin snorted.

Leo chuckled. "I take that as a no. Um. Neither am I, so…"

"Think about it and let me know," Dustin said.

Leo gripped Dustin's wrist to make him look at him, then smiled when they made eye contact. "Yes."

Dustin's cheeks went red. He stuttered for a moment before he managed, "You can think about it, too."

"I don't need to."

Dustin blinked. "I haven't even fucked you yet."

"I don't care. You could be the worst at it and I wouldn't know any different," Leo grinned.

That made Dustin laugh. "I see your point. No pressure, then."

"None," Leo agreed. "Especially for me. I hope I don't suck."

"You won't," Dustin assured him. He cracked the tube of lubricant, spreading wetness across his fingers.

Leo caught his breath and tried not to tense up. He closed his eyes and furrowed his brows. *Relax*, he told himself, which didn't help matters. *Just do it.*

"Kiss me," Dustin murmured, and Leo opened his eyes again to find Dustin hovering over him, his forearm braced next to him on the bed.

Leo smiled. He could do that. He leaned up and met Dustin's lips before Dustin pressed him back to the bed with a series of hot, hard presses of their mouths.

Dustin's fingers slipped between his thighs, and Leo spread his legs, resisting the jolt of nervousness that shuddered through him. But Dustin wasn't sliding his fingers in him yet. He was just circling them gently around the tight hole, teasing the nerves.

Then, Dustin kissed his way slowly down the middle of Leo's body. When Leo realized what he was doing, he moaned Dustin's name again.

Dustin grinned. "Yeah?"

"Little cocktease," Leo muttered, "S'good. You're good."

Dustin's eyes scrunched in that adorable beaming grin of his, and then he kissed the tip of Leo's cock. "See if you call it teasing in a minute."

Leo swallowed hard at the promise in those words. The warm, wet suction of Dustin's mouth around the tip of his cock made it impossible to think up a smart-ass reply. "Oh, fuck," he whispered.

The nerves igniting in his ass were connected to those in the tip of his cock, somehow. His whole body sparked again with electric pleasure as Dustin sucked the tip of his cock into his mouth and slid just the tip of his finger inside at the same moment.

Pinned between Dustin's mouth and hand, he couldn't thrust up or down without a surge of pleasure. Leo took a few moments to gather his wits as Dustin kept his finger still and slowly bobbed his head down, taking his whole shaft in easily.

"Oh, fuck," Leo whispered. He made deep-throating look easy. The sight of his whole length disappearing between Dustin's pretty lips was matched only by the tight sensation of his throat around the tip of Leo's throbbing shaft.

Dustin moaned quietly as he pulled his head up and lapped the tip of his cock. He was working the finger inside slowly now, a little at a time, while his mouth did sinfully incredible things to Leo's hard cock.

By the time Dustin's second finger was sliding inside, Leo was pushing into it. The hunger was inexplicable and all-consuming. He needed to feel their bodies joined together, Dustin hot and hard and pushing inside him.

"Please," Leo whimpered when Dustin's crooked fingers

rubbed his prostate just right, making him throb with pleasure and clench around them. "Oh, fuck. Dustin. Come on."

"You sound about ready now," Dustin murmured teasingly.

"Before I flip you over and ride you into next week," Leo growled.

Dustin moaned. "Hot," he approved. "You can do that later, cowboy. But first…"

The fingers left a void inside Leo—not just physical, but a deeper need to feel Dustin inside him again. He was starting to understand why Dustin felt like being the bottom all the time was greedy. It was fucking *good* in a way nothing else could compare to.

Dustin hurried with the condom and a little extra lube, but even that seemed like an eternity when Leo was waiting for him. He made a mental note to be quicker about it next time he was on top.

And then Dustin crouched over him. His hand on Leo's hip was exactly the grounding touch Leo needed to stay relaxed as Dustin pressed against him. He didn't push inside yet. Just as before, he ground against Leo, his hard shaft sliding between the cheeks, back and forth and around the sensitive hole until Leo was about ready to beg for it.

Leo grabbed Dustin's cheeks and pulled him down for a series of hard kisses, nipping his lower lip and sucking the tip of his tongue until Dustin looked breathless and turned on as hell. "Fuck me," Leo whispered. "Come on. I'm ready."

The heat and pressure gave way to pain for a few moments, and then gradual pleasure. Leo caught his breath, but Dustin rubbed his side, gently reminding him in a whisper to breathe.

And breathe Leo did, burying his head in the side of Dustin's neck and inhaling his scent.

It's Dustin. I trust him. I want this. It'll feel good. He gradually relaxed, calling on the memory from just a minute ago when he couldn't get enough of Dustin's fingers in him.

But this was Dustin's aroused shaft inside him, and it already pressed the sensitive spot inside him in a way that made Leo's toes curl.

The slightest thrust of his hips made the head rub across the spot, and Leo moaned.

"Yeah?" Dustin whispered. "You feel that?"

Leo gulped and nodded sharply. "I feel you. It's good. I didn't… I *get it* now."

When he opened his eyes, Dustin was smiling. He pressed their foreheads together, his lips barely brushing Leo's. "I've never liked this as much as now, either. It's you. That's the difference."

Thank God he said it. A whoosh of breath rushed out of Leo's lungs as he grinned up at Dustin. "Yeah. I was just thinking that."

He didn't have time to ruminate on it, though. Dustin was pushing inside him with one steady thrust at a time until he had a rhythm going. The bed creaked gently under them, and Dustin's hot breaths across his neck and cheek made Leo shudder.

But nothing was as good as the cock surging inside him with careful, measured thrusts. Leo was hard as hell, so much so that it almost ached. He felt full to burst, the pleasure coming with a sharp edge that he recognized from descriptions of prostate orgasms. Everything was different when it was his own body, not something he was reading from a website.

It was completely surreal, but one of the best moments he could remember.

I love him.

It wasn't a revelation—just like a curtain had been drawn back to show him what everything added up to: the trust in him, the desire to know more about him, and the pleasure that came from every innocent touch of his hand and every dirty thrust of his cock deep into Leo's body.

Wherever the hell this was going between them, Leo wanted more.

A grin nearly split his face as he grabbed Dustin and kissed him hard. Dustin went limp in his arms and Leo didn't relent for a moment. He just rolled them over carefully and braced himself on his knees.

It took a moment to figure out the difference when he was on this end, but his hips adjusted to the different movement quickly. Within a few thrusts, he had a quick, hard rhythm going.

Dustin was squirming under him, his hands curled into the sheets on either side of his head. "Fuck, yes! Leo," he panted. "Oh, fuck, that's good."

Leo's pleasure was building up like an electric charge barely contained by his skin, his climax not far off. And it was going to be mindblowing—he could already tell from the way the world narrowed to focus on just Dustin.

Nothing else mattered but crossing that edge, letting Dustin have every bit of his pleasure.

"Come on, baby," Dustin whispered, and then a gentle but firm grip encircled his swollen shaft. "You gonna come on me? Make me yours. Show me how hot you are when you're coming for me."

Leo groaned and threw his head back, clenching hard

around Dustin's shaft. "Yeah!" he urged, and Dustin's grip tightened.

Dustin stroked him a few more times and then Dustin's grip weakened. "I'm—fuck, I can't—" Dustin groaned. "Baby, I'm almost there."

Leo took over, balancing himself with one hand while he stroked himself hard with the other.

A few more thrusts later and he was coming hard enough to cry Dustin's name breathlessly. His heat spilled from him in quick and remarkably strong jets of passion as pleasure crashed recklessly through his body, weakening his limbs.

As he squeezed around Dustin, he felt Dustin shudder and jolt, then cry out under him. Leo opened his eyes again in time to watch his own hand milking himself and Dustin's gaze wandering from his face down to his cock and back, clearly memorizing the sight.

The pleasure Dustin took in the moment only made it that much better for Leo. As Dustin's orgasm hit, his nails dug into Leo's hips and he hissed, rolling his head back against the pillow.

"Yes!" Dustin managed through gritted teeth.

Leo touched his shoulder and chest gently, slowing his pace so he didn't hurt Dustin or himself. He was sensitive all over now, aware of every breeze passing against sweaty skin as he slowly drew himself up and off Dustin, then collapsed on him.

"Fucking… that's… Jesus." Dustin laughed in disbelief, shaking his head.

"What?" Leo murmured, grinning as he gradually settled himself on his forearms over Dustin so he didn't totally crush the smaller man.

Dustin looped his arms around Leo and yanked him

down. Apparently he wanted Leo blanketing him. "I loved that. That's fucking amazing."

"I thought so too," Leo grinned. He barely kept himself from saying, *But I don't know any better.* But Dustin knew that he wasn't much of a bottom—even if he didn't know just how new to it all Leo was. "Is it always like that?"

Dustin snorted with laughter. His spirits were light, and he hadn't stopped smiling. "I've had significantly worse sex. Not with you, though. Yet."

"Give me time. I'll find a way to fuck it up," Leo promised, laughing. He rolled onto his side and drew Dustin against him. "If you want there to be a next time."

Dustin cracked an eye and glared. "Was I not obvious enough? I want you."

Hearing it said so simply yet conclusively... It made Leo's head spin. A pang of jealousy hit him—Dustin knew exactly who he was and what he wanted. He'd figured it out years ago.

But how was Leo to know whether Dustin was the right one for him? He was certain now that he could love Dustin, and that he wanted more. Was he supposed to just date Dustin until things became obvious?

As they lay together, eyes closed and breathing falling into sync, reality started to creep in and nibble at the corners of Leo's happiness.

He would have to come out to his family and friends and coworkers. Over and over again, not just once. His whole identity was shifting—already, he'd caught himself thinking about himself as bi and not straight.

Dustin had crashed into his life totally unexpectedly, and as welcome as it was, being with him meant Leo had to risk it all. If Dustin ever decided to walk away… he wasn't sure he would want another man. Or anyone, really.

Sure, Dustin's heart was on the line, too, but was that enough? Two people afraid of hurting each other?

As Dustin pressed closer to Leo and buried his nose in the crook of Leo's neck, Leo took a deep breath and made a conscious decision to set aside those thoughts.

Yes. For tonight, it would be enough.

CHAPTER
Fifteen

DUSTIN

"Not to be that guy, but you gotta head home." Dustin grinned over his coffee at Leo to soften the blow.

Leo pulled a sad face. "No weekend-long sex-fest this time?"

Dustin crossed his legs and told himself not to let his imagination run wild. He was supposed to want more, not just sex on every surface in the house. "Not this weekend. I have a family thing."

"You're seeing them despite… their weirdness?" Leo asked. He drained his coffee and slid the mug across the counter, then patted down his pockets.

Dustin hummed and nodded noncommittally. He didn't want to get into an argument about whether it was dumb to see his family. His brothers had already made it clear they thought it was. "Got everything?"

"If not, I know where you live," Leo grinned. "Thanks for last night."

Dustin walked him to the door. "No, thank you. It was fun."

"Let me know when you're free, huh?" Leo said lightly.

"Oh, I will," Dustin promised.

Even if they hadn't come to any conclusions about what this was between them, he was positive he wanted it to continue. A week had felt like a long time to wait, which wasn't something he'd experienced with fuck-buddies before. Then again, he hadn't been exclusive with one in a long time.

And the risk was enormous. If he let himself fall for Leo, and Leo got his hopes up and then backed off, Dustin would be crushed. Hell, it was probably too late now. He was committed to *something* with Leo. It just wasn't romance. If he let it become that…

Leo paused by the door, his gaze on Dustin's lips.

His cheeks flushing with heat, Dustin leaned in to quickly close the distance for an awkward kiss. The uncertainty melted away when Leo's hand rose to cup his cheek and Leo gently kissed him back.

"See you soon," Leo murmured. "Good luck."

Dustin managed a quick, "Bye." He held onto the edge of the door while Leo walked down the path to the sidewalk, then caught himself staring after Leo like he was mooning after him or something.

Oh, man. I can't let myself do that. He wasn't going to be the first one to fall—and the one who fell the hardest—all over again. And if he told his brothers, they'd only try to protect him again. It hadn't worked last time, and it wouldn't work this time.

Suddenly, lunch with his family sounded like the perfect distraction. Bring on the horrible match-making attempts. It couldn't be worse than this.

As it turned out, even good old home cooking couldn't take Dustin's mind off the man who had shared his bed last night.

While his mom washed up, his dad was talking about some profitable investment he'd made, which was not only not interesting but pretty damn pointed. Every time they talked, his dad insisted he should start investing part of his salary, without really understanding the reality of life today. His salary wasn't bad, but it was only enough to pay his mortgage and the bills, plus put an emergency savings fund aside—not spring for ten grand in stocks in some company out east.

It wasn't that they were terrible people. They hadn't mistreated him throughout the years. Their insistence that he find some rich man to marry came from a good place of concern for him, he was sure.

It was just… they didn't seem to connect.

But Dustin had never noticed it as acutely as he did now, because he was so used to not connecting with people and keeping to his own little bubble in the corner of any given room.

"Earth to Dustin, come in."

Dustin tuned in just in time to hear his family snickering. His dad was grinning from the recliner, while his mom laughed from the kitchen. His little sister, who still lived at home, was snickering, too.

"That joke got old about two decades ago."

"Oh, someone's cranky today." His dad sounded like he was talking to a toddler. He shook his newspaper and folded it. "I was asking whether you've thought any more about that investment opportunity. My guy will cut you a deal on your fees for the first transaction."

"I'm sure he will." Dustin wondered how much of a kickback his dad would get for referring him. "I dunno. I'll think about it."

His father scowled in irritation and shook his newspaper out again with a sharp snapping sound. "You really need to decide before the opportunity disappears."

Welcome to my life. Dustin jiggled his foot in the air, his ankle over his knee. He'd sat through a painful lunch already —couldn't he leave now? His sense of obligation told him no. "Sure."

"You always do this, you know." That was his mom, drying her hands and sitting next to him on the couch. "Avoid making decisions."

"Is there a point to this round of Let's Lecture Dustin?" Dustin asked, unable to hide the irritation from his voice.

"Well, I was thinking it would be good for you to meet this man." His father spoke with exaggerated patience, and even that seemed calculated to annoy him. "He's a good guy —thirty, which is a bit old for you, but..."

"For real?" Dustin brushed invisible dust off his trousers to give his hands something to do other than ball up into fists like he *was* a toddler throwing a tantrum. "Another man you want to throw me at?"

"He's nice. Has two dogs and a big yard, a good salary, good taste in wine... he's always chatty. You need someone to bring you out of your shell."

"Do I?" Dustin gritted out. "I'm so glad you know what I need in my life."

His mother clicked her tongue. "I don't see what the big

problem is with us trying to set you up with someone. We only want you to be happy."

"But you never listen when I tell you not to do that, which would make me actually happy." Try as he might, Dustin couldn't make it not sound like an accusation.

"I don't see why you have to be so combative about it," his father sighed. "We're trying to set you up with a good thing. Don't you see that?"

"No. You're trying to set me up in your ideal life." Dustin stayed standing up. He wasn't going to sit down and concede another defeat, dooming himself to an afternoon of hearing about the rich gay men his parents were acquainted with.

Seriously, how did they know so many eligible guys? He was starting to suspect they'd joined a professional gay singles' networking club on his behalf.

"You've been avoiding putting any real effort in for years. You go have first dates and then nothing more." His mother shook her head. "If you don't want to end up lonely when you're old…"

"Wow." That was below the belt. Dustin turned and headed for the door. "If you can't respect my choices about my life goals, I shouldn't keep bothering you with my failure to set up a heteronormative family unit according to your mandatory timeframe." He shoved his shoes on while his mother stood up and pursued him. His sister was nowhere to be seen—probably hiding in the kitchen and listening in.

"I don't see why you're making such a big deal of it, Dustin. If you don't like men, just say so. We'll find women for you to settle down with."

He reeled, stinging like he'd been slapped. "What did you say to me?"

"I know, I know. Nobody ever acknowledges someone

might like *both*. But if you do, that's fine with us. We'll respect that choice."

Dustin grabbed his jacket and shoved it on, his heart hammering as he pulled open the door and slammed it behind himself.

He didn't care about coming off as mature anymore. He was too angry to even form words in response. Using *that* against him, like being bi was such a terrible thing they were hard-pressed to accept—like it was a choice—like he hadn't made it clear that he was only interested in men, but none of the ones they found for him...

Dustin's driving on his way home was less than safe. He was so wound up he stuck to the roads he knew by heart, so he hardly had to think about when to brake for stop signs or traffic lights.

"How fucking dare they?" he finally hissed as he shut off the car, staring up at the path to his front door. He'd already missed two phone calls from his parents' home phone number.

And no wonder. Storming out was not his style—he'd never been prone to dramatics at all—but what the hell else was he supposed to do? Stay and bash his head against that brick wall?

Oh, fuck. He felt... overshadowed. That was the word.

Like everyone around him was trying to make decisions for him, or protect him, or set him up with the future they wanted. All with the best intentions, sure, but that didn't the change the fact that it wasn't *his* decision.

Maybe they were right. He'd avoided making decisions for a long time, afraid of pissing people off. It was easier to just quietly say "maybe" and not get around to doing things.

Fine. It was time to decide what he wanted and fucking

own it. Time to stand on his own two feet. Time to figure out what he was so afraid of and conquer it.

Time to man up and be the man they'd always wanted him to be instead of the shy, quiet nerd in the corner—but for his own sake. Nobody else's.

For that matter, he needed hobbies. Things to do that weren't either drowning himself in work or visiting his parents every weekend like a good little obedient son, even when they insulted him to his face.

As he slammed his own front door and locked it, he set the contents of his pockets on the table by the door as always, glancing at his phone.

Oh. One of the missed notifications wasn't from his parents at all. It was the group text thread, and reading the message didn't improve his mood at all.

Valentine's Day coming up! I've got a great idea for us all. +1s mandatory. Looking at you Josh, Tyler, Dustin. No stress, bring a fuckbuddy if you want. ;) 6pm, meet in front of the usual bar but plan for something else first. No spoilers! xoxo.

It was from the sometimes insufferably perky Falcon, Blane's boyfriend. No doubt he thought of himself as a matchmaker now that his best friend was happily set up with Roman.

That's right. Valentine's Day is only... what, a week away? Oh, fuck me. There's no way around this.

He plopped on the couch and thumped the phone against his forehead. Now that he'd brought up exclusivity and Leo had sounded on board, he wasn't about to hop on Grindr and find some stranger.

Which, logically, meant asking Leo to be a plus-one or else finding an excuse to skip the night. Work was always a convenient excuse, but hadn't he just thought a minute ago that he needed to get out and do hobbies and not lose himself in work all the time?

He'd have to ask Leo out, then.

Which meant putting his heart on the line—in front of everyone. If it went wrong, he wasn't going to let the guys shake down Leo, either. It was time to stop letting them run things, too, however good their intentions. So maybe they were right that Leo was worth pursuing, but it had to be his decision.

The next step was clear: logically, he had to call Leo and ask about Valentine's Day plans. That was supposed to be easy, right? With his new, improved confidence and go-get-'em attitude?

Dustin's hand shook as he stared down at the phone.

Yeah, it's too late. My heart's already on the line.

He could wait a little while. Ask at work, maybe.

Yeah. He'd ask when he saw Leo next. Surely he could find the right time this week.

CHAPTER
Sixteen

LEO

I T WAS ONLY T UESDAY, BUT L EO WAS EXHAUSTED.

"You wanna do something after work?"

That sure as hell wasn't going to help matters. He pushed back the urge to sigh, instead giving Victor a polite smile. "What were you thinking?"

"Go out for drinks, cruise for chicks… the old days."

Those weren't like any old days Leo remembered, but Victor seemed to be reminiscing every time they bumped into each other at the station or even at a scene. Letting him get it out of his system might help.

"Okay, sure. When? Today?"

"Sure, man!" Victor grinned, but the expression felt like a challenge rather than an invitation. "Or do you already have plans?"

Leo hadn't seen Dustin at work on Monday, since he'd been off and at school all day. Today, their paths hadn't crossed once yet. Safe to say there were no plans yet, although Leo kind of wanted there to be. "What? No."

"Good, good." Victor leaned into Leo's cubicle, his thumb

hooked through his belt. "You know what the guys have been saying, right?"

"About me?" Leo asked, folding his arms as he leaned back in his office chair. He had a pretty damn good idea, and he was also pretty sure Victor was full of it. He hadn't heard whispers about himself, and he hadn't even seen any sideways glances. "Shoot."

"Well, uh… you know. You're back in town a little different now."

"Spit it out. You think I'm gay?"

Victor almost choked. "I didn't say that, man," he said, holding his palms out and up, facing Leo. Like he was trying to apologize or calm him down… like it was an insult, even.

"It's not an insult," Leo told him. "Just a statement of fact. Not a true fact, but there you are."

"Oh." Victor's chest swelled as if with relief. "I mean, cool. Nobody cares around here."

"But they still talk about it?" Leo challenged.

Victor cleared his throat. "Well, you know. You came to that cake auction with Dustin—you two baked a *cake* together." He snickered.

"You know, you missed an important question," Leo said. He grabbed his empty coffee mug and shouldered past Victor, but the annoying prick followed him to the lunch room.

"What's that?"

"It's not that important to you if you didn't think about it." Leo pointedly glanced toward the forensics lab as they passed that hallway.

Victor's brow furrowed. "Are you buddies with Dustin?"

Leo almost laughed. *It's like bi doesn't even exist in their minds. God, it probably doesn't in his.* "Sure. Yeah. He's probably my best friend in town right now."

"Ah, man. You could have told me!" Victor insisted, shadowing him all the way to the coffee maker as he set down his mug and grabbed a second mug. "I didn't realize you weren't settling in."

"I am. I don't need pity dates, even of the friendship variety," Leo said drily. "So, you want drinks tonight? But only if I'm not gay?"

"Oh, I never said *that*. I just don't want people thinking it's more than it is."

Leo's lips quirked. "Man, you could walk into a gay bar and everyone there would know you're straight. You got nothing to worry about."

Victor took it as a compliment. He stood straighter, his thumbs returning to his belt like they were supposed to be holstered there. "Right. Right," he said to himself. "So come grab me on your way out of the place."

"Right you are. No coffee for me, thanks. I'm quitting."

"Sure," Leo answered, pouring the second mug of coffee as he listened to Victor's retreating footsteps. He shook his head. Victor really had always been that bad, he was willing to bet.

A few minutes later, in the doorway of the forensics lab, he paused. It was awkward to try to knock on the door with a mug of coffee in each hand, so he swayed from side to side for a moment like a fucking willow in the wind.

Dustin looked like he was deep in thought, staring at the computer monitor like he hadn't seen or heard a thing. But just as Leo was about to clear his throat, his nostrils flared. "Coffee? Who's bribing me today?"

"I wouldn't call it a bribe," Leo answered coyly. He

slowly approached Dustin, and Dustin's eyes quickly turned to his. He noted that speed with which Dustin's attention shifted to him. Surely that was a good thing, right?

"Oh. Then what is it?"

"A good-will gesture?" Leo winked. "Since I haven't seen you in a while."

Dustin smirked. "A whole day and a half." He lowered his voice, though, to that covert half-whisper that they used when they were referencing their out-of-office shenanigans.

"It feels like a fucking long time," Leo admitted. He set down Dustin's mug next to him, but kept an appropriate distance away as he studied the images on the screen.

These weren't anything like the photos he was used to taking. Fine-grain, high-definition images of… what the hell was that, even?

"Cotton," Dustin answered the unasked question. "I'm trying to figure out if it's twine or something else." His eyes strayed back to the screen, his brow furrowing. "The pattern is consistent…" he trailed off in a murmur, sounding like he was composing a report in his head.

Leo figured Dustin could use a distraction from the grim pictures on the desk. "So, you'll never guess who asked me out," he said with a smile.

Dustin nearly spilled the coffee. He sucked in a quick breath and checked the front of his lab coat, then looked up at Leo. "Who?"

The reaction said more than Dustin had probably meant to. Leo tried to hide the pleasure. "Victor."

"*What?*"

"As a friend. Guy to guy. Mano-a-mano. Just two bros being bros." Leo rolled his eyes. "Need I go on?"

"Oh, Jesus," Dustin muttered under his breath. "Just tell him to fuck off back to his hillbilly tribe."

"I'm gonna venture a guess that you guys don't get along these days, either."

"Luckily, he ain't in charge of anything," Dustin answered carefully. "So management here has *some* sense. I don't usually deal directly with him."

"Taking that as a yes." Leo sipped his coffee, breathing in the wonderful scent. "So we're doing drinks tonight."

"We—oh. You and Victor." Dustin smiled tightly and looked back at the screen. "That'll be fun."

Leo hesitated. "I'd ask if you wanna come along, but…"

"Dangle the bait a little closer to the lion's mouth, why don't you?" Dustin asked, but he didn't sound angry. It was a dry, sarcastic sort of comment hiding something else that Dustin wasn't letting him in on.

Leo was getting another call. "Damn it. Crime never takes a break, does it?"

Dustin looked back at him, the air instantly clearer between them. He seemed sincere as he said, "Good luck."

"Thanks."

"Get me some clear photos."

Leo saluted with his mug and drained the remnants as he headed for his desk to grab his gear. Before he got to the scene, nobody could touch a thing. So time was always of the essence.

Even when he had a half-unsaid conversation to finish with Dustin.

"Turned out to be a damn vehicular break-and-enter. Nothing out of the ordinary," Leo said. He licked the head from the edge of the glass as he took that first delicious sip of his third beer.

"Good. Great," Victor answered, his eyes on the bartender. She looked exactly his type, from what Leo remembered. This was going to be a long, boring night if Victor was serious about chasing chicks.

"So, tell me what's new," Leo pressed, trying to change the course of events before he wound up losing his mind from boredom and playing wingman to a cocky asshole he didn't really like anymore.

He hadn't even had another chance to talk to Dustin. By the time he'd documented the scene, Dustin had gone home, leaving him to collect Victor and head for the bar.

Ugh. If this was what having a social life was like, he'd take being a loner.

"Huh? Oh," Victor looked back at him, sipping his beer. "Not a whole lot, I gotta be honest, man. It's not like you. Shipped all 'round the world, being a hero and shit. Some of us gotta keep working the beat. The small-time cases. Keeping law and order."

Leo's brows furrowed. "That's the other thing. Since when were you all law and order?"

"You remember my dad, right?"

Ohhh. Leo had nearly forgotten: Victor's dad had been the sheriff. "He retired now?"

"Yep. But he wanted to get his boy in. The new sheriff hand-picked me," Victor bragged.

Leo didn't think much of that recommendation since Victor had apparently stayed in the same job for the last few years with no plans of changing that, but ambition had never been Victor's strong suit. Come to think of it, what had been? Coasting by and copying others' work?

"So, how'd you get into the photography side of things? It looks kinda interesting. And a lot easier than chasing perps."

There it was. Victor was hoping for the sweet gig—the easy job.

Fighting back irritation and the urge to tell him how much technical knowledge went into every shot, Leo shrugged. "You know I was always taking pictures. Military wanted me to do it. They taught me a lot. Came back, the job was open, they sent me for a quick course, and then I started in November."

"That's like… two, three months? You liking it?" Victor asked. "It as easy as it looks?"

"I like it enough, but no. It's pretty hard. A lot of different technical shit. It's not just iPhone cameras," Leo told Victor.

"Yeah. Yeah," Victor hummed, leaning back on his bar stool. "How would I get into something like that?"

"Start with a photography class, I guess. Learn the basics. They use digital now, but knowing your darkroom basics will teach you the fundamentals."

"Digital's easy. I like digital," Victor said as if he hadn't heard him. "They probably do digital photography classes. Say, you're at the college, aren't you?"

How the hell he knew that, Leo had no idea. "Yeah. Part-time classes. The bosses here are great about working with me."

"How are those college chicks?"

"Very eighteen," Leo said pointedly, but that didn't seem to deter Victor, so he added, "so I dunno. That'd be pretty creepy. I'm sure as hell not in their league."

"Oh, come on. Don't put yourself down, man. War hero,

police hero, you've got every stripe of hero." Several beers down, Victor was the worse for wear already. "The heroes, man. They like the heroes."

"And they're all dating each other like they should be," Leo said. "Being idiots while they're young and green. Learning how to hold down a relationship. Speaking of which…"

"Nah, man. None of that ball-and-chain for me," Victor waved dismissively. "Too much sweet candy out there to stick to one lollipop."

Leo shook his head and snorted. "Yeah? And when you're thirty-something and you've never had a serious relationship? I mean, learning that shit late is hard."

"You thinking about dating?" Victor asked. He swayed slightly, looking at Leo.

"Thinking about it," Leo echoed. "Yeah. But I'm learning to even, you know, make friends in class. That kind of shit. I never really took the time. The military throws a bunch of you together and you're workmates and buddies right away. A couple of mature students have a club or whatever, though. Coffee club. They asked me yesterday if I wanna join. It's weird, though. They're all coming back to school after degrees or kids or whatever. And then there's the freshman. I'm like… in-between."

God, it was nice to vent, even if he didn't feel like he could fully trust Victor.

"That's rough." Victor didn't have any particular conviction in his voice.

But more importantly, it gave Leo the chance to say, "So I might not be able to hang out much. Between homework and now… I dunno, this society… and work and everything."

"Oh, no. You do you, man." Victor hiccupped. "Hey, when that chick bends over, you can see her nips."

"Cool." Leo stared into the distance and drank up faster.

It was the most stilted conversation he'd had with a supposed friend in ages, but it at least confirmed that he had no interest in being friends with this guy anymore.

As long as he wasn't gonna cause trouble when it came out that he and Dustin were together, he was happy to leave this friendship where it belonged: the past.

He had other, newer, better friendships waiting for him. Starting with Dustin, but not finishing there.

The more people he had around him, the better.

"Wonder if she's doing anything for V-Day. You know," Victor promised when Leo stared blankly. "Valentine's."

Leo snorted again. "That's not what that means in my world. Yeah. She's got a ring on, so I bet she is."

"Oh. Shit," Victor sighed. "Why are the hot ones always taken?"

Wait... He said Valentine's. "Man, what day is it this year?"

"Next Wednesday. You and me, man," Victor said, jabbing a finger into Leo's chest. "We'll go out on the prowl. Pick up some lonely singles. It'll be great. Yeah!"

"Maybe," Leo hedged. He swallowed the rest of his beer so fast his throat burned. "Anyway, I gotta run. Work tomorrow."

"Fucking work." Victor slapped his back and gave him a thumbs-up. "See ya, man."

"See you."

Leo had never been so glad to walk out of a bar. He shook his head as he hailed a car, not caring how long he had to wait on the sidewalk as long as he didn't have to listen to that guy anymore.

The one useful thing he'd said all night was two words: *Valentine's Day.*

What was Dustin thinking about it? Was it weird to acknowledge it? Hell, they weren't even officially together. They'd just kinda-sorta agreed not to sleep with other people. That didn't even mean dating yet.

He'd never experienced the awkward early dating stage where Valentine's Day was way too soon and neither person knew whether to acknowledge it, but it suddenly hit him.

We're gonna have to talk about this.

If only he weren't off work for the next couple days—lies to Victor to get out of there aside.

That meant a text or a phone call, which were even more awkward.

Maybe he'd let it go until Friday. Make it casual, like he'd forgotten the day was coming up. They could do something last-minute and low-pressure.

Yeah. Low-pressure sounded great to him.

CHAPTER
Seventeen

DUSTIN

FRIDAY AFTERNOON, AND THERE WAS NO WAY DUSTIN WAS walking out until he'd talked to Leo. After all, Dustin had just happened to notice on the schedule that Leo was working that day.

He couldn't wait any longer to do it. Leo probably had to arrange to take the evening off, so Dustin had to give him notice. Plus, his brothers kept nagging him about whether he had a date. He could only put them off for so long. If he was going to make an excuse about working, it couldn't be last-minute, or they'd see through it.

It felt like he was living inside his own head as he argued the merits of talking to Leo—just asking one simple, easy question

Do you wanna meet my brothers?

Jesus. He'd never thought of himself as especially shy, just in comparison to his brothers. But now? The idea of talking to Leo, asking him to meet his best friends in the world, was utterly terrifying.

Maybe some of it did come down to his dating history. Which, if they dated, he was going to have to tell the guy, too. He'd already spilled enough of it accidentally, it would probably come out on its own if he didn't.

He jumped when a voice in the doorway said his name.

"Whoa. Sorry." Leo was carrying two mugs of coffee.

"Again? I'm starting to suspect you're lacing that." Dustin grinned, then winced. Wow. That was the least romantic thing he'd said. Not the best way to start.

"With a little love potion number nine? It doesn't smell like turpentine or look like Indian ink. I think you're safe." Leo grinned back and handed over the mug.

Dustin awkwardly smiled, and everything he'd planned to say about Valentine's Day vanished in his mouth. "Uh. So. Cool. Hi. Thanks."

Leo, seemingly unfazed by his suddenly being tongue-tied, smiled back. "Hey. No problem."

"Long time no see," Dustin mumbled. *I could wait until the weekend, right? See him on Saturday or Sunday, ask him on Wednesday...*

"Yeah. Yeah, it's felt like a long time… again," Leo grinned teasingly. "What's on your mind?"

Oh, man. Dustin swallowed hard and glanced at his computer screen. No escape there. "Uh. Slow day at work."

"Uh huh. For me, too. I like those days." Leo sipped his coffee, reminding Dustin to drink his own.

Dustin nearly scalded his tongue in his haste to cover up his own awkwardness. "Ow. Fuck."

"Sorry. Shit, I should have warned you."

Dustin mumbled, "You can kiss it better this weekend. If you want."

"I was just coming to see if you had Friday night plans." Leo winked. "I swear I didn't set that up, though. I'd be delighted to provide medical first response… this evening."

"Definitely not at work," Dustin nodded.

"No. For sure."

"Too many eyes," Dustin said.

"Yeah."

"I'm not even sure our policies on those things."

Leo grinned at him. "What has you so flustered all of a sudden?"

It was a good question. Dustin was normally able to stay reserved and cool at work, or even outside work, with everyone around him. The only explanation—that there was something different about Leo—was something he couldn't exactly say at work.

So he just mumbled, "Long week."

"Wanna come over after work and talk?"

"Yes," Dustin answered so fast it embarrassed him. "I mean, yeah. We should chat."

Leo's lips quirked into an amused grin. "I was thinking that too. We left some things hanging there."

"For a whole week," Dustin nodded.

"Uh huh. Sorry about that. Things have been crazy with school and whatnot," Leo shook his head. "And I wasn't sure how you felt about me texting you… you know. Off-hours."

"Why not?" Dustin shook his head. "We didn't meet at work, after all."

Leo blinked. "That's a good point."

"And if it's not talking about work stuff…" Dustin trailed off meaningfully.

"No. It isn't." It was Leo's turn to look nervous, and perhaps a bit shifty. "Yeah, we'll talk tonight, huh?"

"Tonight. Six? At your place?" Dustin asked.

"Want me to pick you up?"

"No, no." Dustin figured he should have his own way home, in case they didn't end up… just sleeping together. Again. As usual. "I'll drive there."

Leo smiled and nodded. "Cool. See you later."

Dustin waved, then cringed at himself as he wrapped his hands around the mug and blew on the hot coffee.

Ugh. That was the most awkward conversation ever. Hopefully tonight's didn't beat it.

The hours crept by. By the time Dustin headed home, he had an elaborate script in his head.

He had to explain that his brothers weren't really looking for him to have a boyfriend, just a plus-one, so if Leo didn't want to date that was cool. And if he wanted to tell them he was straight, they'd be fine with that.

It did mean being seen in public with all of them and he couldn't control people's assumptions—by people, he meant Victor—but Leo seemed kind of okay about that, compared to most straight guys. Or bi guys. Newly-out guys. New gays.

But everything vanished when he arrived on Leo's doorstep and the guy answered the door in a freaking clingy t-shirt that showed off all his muscles. By the grin he gave Dustin, he knew exactly what he was doing.

"Uh. Hi," Dustin managed.

"Come on in." Leo held the door for him, making him brush past him on the way past. Both of them shivered at the touch—they were close enough he could feel Leo's reaction.

Leo didn't let him get further than the entryway before wrapping an arm around his waist. "I missed you."

"I missed you, too," Dustin admitted. With Leo's arm around him, the layers of uncertainty and professionalism and attempted friendship melted away, and they were back to who they had been on the night they'd met.

Leo drew him in for a kiss and Dustin pressed close to him, finally wrapping his arms around Leo's shoulders as he returned it. Their warm lips slid together in a short but sweet dance.

Then Leo pulled back and smiled. "Come in, then." He caught Dustin by the hand and tugged him into the living room.

Dustin's uncertainty about Leo's label and what that meant for him melted away whenever Leo treated him like this. It was only in private so far, with guarded hints in public, but Leo seemed willing to look past whatever had held him back from men before.

"Sorry things were so weird at work this week," Dustin found himself apologizing.

"No, no. It's our workplace. They're bound to be weird sometimes." Leo smiled crookedly. "Especially with Victor around. I'm not hanging out with him again. Jesus, the guy is self-centered."

"Told you so," Dustin couldn't resist muttering, and Leo laughed.

"Yeah, you did. I'm thinking you're a lot smarter than you let on. Drink?"

Dustin blushed and shrugged. "Water's fine." Alcohol might help him extend the invitation, but he wanted a clear head to talk about… everything else surrounding it, too.

"So," Leo said when he came back with a couple glasses of

water and settled next to Dustin on the couch. "Next week. Valentine's Day."

Dustin exhaled so deeply his lungs almost hurt. "Oh, thank God."

Leo laughed richly. "What? Was it bothering you, too?"

"Yes! I've been trying to ask for, like, a week," Dustin admitted, his cheeks hot. "But I thought it might be… I don't know. Weird."

"Because we're not officially boyfriends, but we were talking monogamy already, and… in that awkward in-between stage?"

Dustin stared at Leo. "Don't beat around the bush." He laughed, though, to show he didn't mind. "I like that we both think similarly. It's like you're writing a report."

"They've got me well-trained already." Leo shook his head. "So, speaking of those problems… I guess we start with the boyfriend thing?"

"I've been wanting to ask." Dustin sighed. "But with you being… I don't know… not gay?"

Leo chuckled quietly. "I never said, did I?" He looked like he knew exactly what he hadn't said. "Okay. I always called myself straight, but not because I was hiding. I've dated women. I didn't mind them. I didn't particularly want to spend my life with any of them, but it wasn't like I knew they weren't for me."

"Right. Which I did, pretty early," Dustin smiled.

"Exactly. So then… I don't know. You came along, and I saw you and it just felt right. And I figure, fuck it, life is too short to worry about other people's bullshit boxes. Since then I've been thinking bi is the right word for me. I don't mind women, I don't mind men. I want a person I can… I can talk to, I can trust," Leo said, his words becoming more halting, but no less sincere.

Dustin slipped his hand into Leo's and set aside his glass of water. "No, I get it," he assured him. "I mean, I know I'm not attracted to women, but I feel that way about men. I'm not just going to date anyone."

Leo lit up. "Yeah! Nobody ever says that, you know. I mean, not the guys I hang out with."

"My friends are pretty cool. Actually, if you wanna meet them soon… but we'll finish this conversation first," Dustin laughed.

Leo pretended to gulp. "Uh oh. Friend vetting."

Dustin grinned. "Nah. You'll be fine," he assured Leo. A guy as easygoing and coolheaded as Leo could get along with them, he was sure. Hell, if he could get along with Victor, he could get along with anyone. As long as he could stand a little teasing.

"But yeah, nobody says they're waiting for the right one. They just seem to kind of dive from relationship to relationship," Leo said slowly. "Most of my friends, anyway. I never wanted that. I've always had… a strict career, and things I want to do. I guess I felt lonely sometimes, but I just knew I should wait."

Dustin felt a pang of sympathy for him when he admitted loneliness. "Me too. I mean, I've waited because… Well. I've been scared for a long time of getting my heart broken by some loser like I did in high school," he breathily chuckled, ignoring the sting of painful truth. "But also, same thing. Hooking up with men is one thing. Dating means… I want to actually like you."

"And you don't like a lot of people?" Leo grinned.

Dustin blushed. "Uh. If you wanna put it that way…"

"You seem a little… reclusive?" Leo guessed. "You know. Shy, quiet, would rather keep to himself than hang out with idiots."

Dustin laughed at this sharp perception. "I guess you could say that, too."

"I respect that," Leo added. "I've been a bit too quick to accept friendship in the past." *And the present.*

Dustin scooted over until he leaned into Leo, and Leo wrapped his arm around his shoulder. "Yeah?"

"I need people around, I think." Leo shook his head. "It sounds dumb, but since I moved here, I've been… wilting, a little. Talking to you has helped a lot. I'm starting to make friends again."

"You seem brighter," Dustin offered. That was what had annoyed him so much in the lab earlier that week: the prospect of hanging out with Victor had clearly annoyed Leo, but he'd also been brighter and more energetic. Goddamn extroverts.

"Yeah." Leo gazed at Dustin, then bit his lip. "So, uh. The whole… seeing other people thing."

"I haven't hooked up with anyone since you," Dustin said frankly. He didn't see the point in beating around the bush. "I *could*, but the sex with you is good, and I've been bored with assholes who can't bother to put effort in lately."

Leo laughed. "Yeah. I… Well. You've shown me totally new things."

"Like bottoming?"

For a moment, Leo looked shy. It was an adorable look on a man big enough to snap him like a twig. "Yeah, like that."

"Did you like it? You seemed to," Dustin told him.

"It's good. It's really—I mean, I see why you like it now. I think I'd still rather be inside you, but… it's a different orgasm. I've… uh, played around a little more since. With myself. I haven't hooked up with anyone else," Leo added so hastily that Dustin grinned.

"So, if we're not fucking others, we might as well date," Dustin stated.

Leo started to laugh.

"What?"

Leo cleared his throat, trying to look innocent. "Nothing."

"Tell me," Dustin said with a vaguely threatening glare, walking two fingers along Leo's ribs. "Or I tickle."

"Good luck with that," Leo snorted and batted his hand away. "I was just thinking that you're very… um… practical."

Dustin bit his lip, his hand resting on Leo's leg now. "Is that bad?"

"No! God, no. I lo—I mean, it's adorable," Leo said, with maybe more enthusiasm than he meant to let slip, judging by his blush a moment later. "I don't think romances built on, like, fairytale dreams will last."

Dustin glanced away. "No. They don't." If his experiences had hardened him, at least it wasn't unattractive to a practical guy like Leo. Maybe he had a chance after all.

Leo's tone was soft. "I like that about you, and I like you. If you're willing to take me on board given that I'm, uh, new to all this guy stuff…"

"You're not bad at it," Dustin winked. "I'll date you. But I don't want to pressure you just because there's a holiday coming up. We've still hardly even seen each other, you know?"

Leo hummed, rubbing Dustin's shoulder. "Okay. There's an idea: actually seeing each other more. Talking to each other outside work, texting. Trying this out as a romance and not just a friendship."

Dustin swallowed hard. There was the commitment, and the potential heartbreak, in a sentence. His voice almost wavered, but he kept it steady with all his willpower. "Are you serious about this? Me?"

"Yeah. Are you?" Leo asked, his gaze searching Dustin's.

Why wouldn't I be? Then, Dustin realized that Leo might just be thinking the same thing himself. He half-grinned. "Fair enough. Yeah. I am, too."

"Then we'll try dating—going steady? And if things go well, we can talk about being boyfriends and… you know, how to handle work…" Leo shook his head. "And family, and all that shit."

"Going steady," Dustin repeated. That sounded nice. Sweetly old-fashioned, even. "Yeah. Let's do that. And Valentine's Day… I have something to ask you."

"Go for it."

"Do you wanna be my plus-one? And meet my brothers?"

Leo gazed at Dustin, and the anxiety in his eyes was enough to warm Dustin's heart. "You think they'll like me?"

"Why do you ask?" Dustin realized a moment later where it was coming from. "Oh. Because of them scaring off my beaus before?"

Leo crookedly grinned. "Not that I can't hold my own, but if they're protecting your virtue…"

"They're much too late," Dustin snorted, squeezing Leo's thigh meaningfully. "And no, they won't test you like they're, I dunno. Creepy fathers." He laughed. "They know I've got good judgment. I think they'll be happy I'm not just withering away waiting for a Prince Charming."

Leo leaned in and pressed a kiss to his lips. "Then sure. Let's go be each other's Prince Charming." The next sentence out of his mouth made Dustin fall for him perhaps more than anything else, especially spoken with that crooked *fuck-'em-all* attitude. "Why the hell not?"

I need to learn to live a little. Dustin straightened up, his heart racing. *Push my boundaries. Choose for myself. He's right.* "We've got nothing to lose."

CHAPTER
Eighteen
LEO

Despite his bold words last weekend, Leo's palms were sweating enough to lubricate a whole army of cocks. He wiped his hands on his trousers as he pulled up in front of Dustin's house, but it wouldn't last long.

Just another Wednesday evening, he told himself, but he knew it was fucking untrue. It was Valentine's Day, and he was going to meet the people most important to Dustin.

He couldn't fuck this up.

"Hey!" Dustin looked adorable as always, but a peek at his neck showed he was wearing a tie today.

"Oh, shit. Did I underdress?" Leo had thought the white shirt and suit jacket were a little over-the-top, but apparently not.

Dustin's eyes swept up and down Leo in a way that made him hastily think unsexy thoughts. "No," Dustin answered after a moment and grinned. "That's perfect."

Leo cleared his throat and willed his cock to stand down. "Good. I mean, you're all sexy there with your sweater and tie. I don't want to be the slob on your arm you randomly picked up on your way."

Dustin's laugh always brightened Leo's day. The whole-hearted joy and playfulness he hid behind that serious exterior felt like a secret he'd painstakingly uncovered, and he cherished it.

Dustin leaned over the center console and pecked Leo's lips in a quick kiss. "Happy Valentine's Day to a handsome hunk I picked up in a bar."

The blush was painfully obvious even to Leo. Dustin laughed as his cheeks heated up, and Leo waved a hand at him as he pulled away from the curb. "Oh, stop."

"Never. I thought I was the only one who went tomato-red, but apparently it's not just a saying."

Leo snorted and swatted Dustin's arm. "You're a handful."

"Two, later." Dustin snuck a pinch to Leo's ass, working his hand between the seatbelt and seat.

"Oh, you're several handfuls," Leo revised with a laugh. "So, what's up tonight?"

"Now that the plan finally isn't secret..." Dustin rolled his eyes. "Tapas, sangria, and painting."

"Very multicultural." It actually sounded like a cute idea. "Are all your brothers gonna be there? And plus-ones?"

"Yeah. Most of them are in relationships now... two aren't, so God knows what they're going to do. I think this was all a plot," Dustin shook his head.

Leo glanced over. "To get you dating?"

"I *really* don't want to admit it might have worked," Dustin laughed.

"Then we won't tell them a thing," Leo winked. "How do you want to say we met?" His hand rested on the stick, even though it was an automatic car.

"Oh, we can tell them at a bar. They won't judge." Dustin grinned, sliding his hand over Leo's. "And they'll like you, so relax." The warmth and pressure reassured him that he wasn't about to be interrogated by a mob family.

"I hope you're right." Leo hadn't met anyone's family in… well, ever. Meeting chosen family seemed even more stressful, because these were people who had taken Dustin as a brother without any obligation. There were few stronger bonds than that of freely chosen loyalty.

Leo's phone went off in the cup holder, but he ignored it. Dustin's eyes, however, strayed down to the screen, and then he tensed up. He didn't pull away from Leo's hand, but there was a sudden air of caution, too.

As he pulled up to a red light, Leo glanced down at the screen in time to see Victor's name come up on the missed call display. "Ah, shit."

"Didn't ditch plans with him to be with me, did you?" Dustin's chuckle sounded forced.

"I figured he was talking out of his ass when he was drunk." Leo scratched his neck as he glanced over at Dustin. "Last time we hung out, he said we should go hunt singles or something."

"Well, you've caught one." The light turned green and Leo had to glance away from Dustin. "What are you going to do with him?"

"Oh, I had *plenty* of ideas for later," Leo growled playfully, turning his hand over to catch Dustin's arm. He pulled Dustin's hand to his mouth and kissed it, then pretended to nibble his arm.

It worked—Dustin relaxed and giggled. "Silly."

"I aim to please."

Dustin pulled his hand free and ran it up Leo's arm. "Me too."

"Oh, now you're going to get me very distracted while I try to parallel-park."

"Expert-level parking. Impress me," Dustin teased, but he pulled his hand back.

Leo smirked, trying to focus on the points of his car as he tucked it into the parking spot. If sangria was on the menu, it was going to be another Uber today. He was going to become one of their best customers any time now, after never having taken one before he moved back here just a couple months ago.

"Nice," Dustin whistled under his breath. "A man with hand-eye coordination."

"I've proven that already in oral arguments."

Dustin laughed again, unbuckling so he could lean over and kiss Leo.

If that was what a clever joke got him, Leo was going to spend his idle courtroom minutes thinking them up. And maybe his idle classroom minutes.

Which reminded him again that it was Wednesday, so he had a short paper due tomorrow. Time just slipped away between one thing and another. Besides, this was more important.

His phone rang again, and Leo cursed under his breath. Of course Victor wasn't leaving him alone. "Hold on a sec. Let me get him off my back," he told Dustin.

"Sure," Dustin answered and slid out of the car.

Leo hurried to grab his phone and answer while unbuckling his seatbelt. He kept his voice brisk. "Hello."

"Hey, man. What's up? It's hunting season."

"Sorry, man. I got a hot date of my own tonight." Leo didn't even care what came of this. "Have fun."

"Ah, man. Bros before hos," Victor complained. "What's up with that?"

"Hey, can't say you didn't see it coming. Talk to you later." Leo hung up and grinned to himself. That was going to drive Victor nuts. He might not even see him until that weekend, if tomorrow was a quiet night in Knoxville PD.

He hopped out of the car and locked it up with a cheery grin as he silenced his phone and pocketed it. "All ready."

"Okay. It's just around the corner." Dustin walked close to him as he directed them to what looked like a little café. There were paper decorations and streamers in the windows, and a chalk board outside advertising their Valentine's Day party.

A couple guys already stood around outside, one of them holding hands with another. Leo guessed those might be Dustin's brothers.

"Blane! Falcon! Hey," Dustin called out with a grin, probably for Leo's benefit.

"Oh, you did find yourself a date after all!" The smaller of the two guys looked delighted. He leaned in to hug Leo, air-kissing his cheeks. "Falcon. This is Blane, my boyfriend."

Leo shook hands with Blane, and then he found himself the center of attention as they were steered into the cafe. Half a dozen or more guys were already there.

One by one, he met the others: Nico, a big guy dressed in plaid who looked a little uncomfortable in the artsy space; Deen, vaguely familiar and wearing dark eyeliner; Roman, boisterous and cheerful; Oscar, already wearing a smock over a sweater with colorful paint-like splotches.

"And those idiots are Tyler and Josh."

They were both wearing fake glasses—the plastic kind with mustaches built in. Before he could ask, Josh whipped his glasses off. "I'm Josh, that's Tyler." He put them back on after shaking hands. "And I'm Not-Josh, Tyler's date."

"Cheating cheaters," Falcon muttered, but Oscar was cracking up too much to breathe. "They were supposed to bring a date…"

Leo grinned as he got it. "Well, maybe they did."

"That's right," Not-Josh said, resting his head on Tyler's shoulder and batting his lashes. "Isn't it, darling? They shouldn't mock our romance."

Blane plucked the glasses off Josh's face and shook his head. "Losers couldn't even find a date for one night."

"Dustin followed the rules," Roman agreed, straightening his face as he shook his head. "And brought a very nice gentleman date."

Tyler cleared his throat and tried for a contrite look, but he was smirking too much. "That sounded like effort."

"Why do I get the feeling they didn't even try?" Falcon rolled his eyes.

"Since when have we ever followed the rules?" Josh said.

Falcon clicked his tongue. "Now that we're all here, with our dates," he said with a severe stare in their direction, "these lovely people have tapas for us." The place was set up with stools in two rows facing each other, tables between them. "We're going to eat before we start painting and probably get paint all over ourselves."

While the heckling continued for Josh and Tyler, Leo took a moment to look around and remind himself of people's names. He was sitting opposite his date, next to Josh and Tyler, with Roman and Oscar on the other side. There were other couples there, too, but the brothers had claimed one end of the area for themselves.

"So, everyone's going to be looking at you two," Oscar warned, leaning in to murmur with a grin. "Since Josh and Tyler neatly avoided that trap."

Leo gulped. "Uh oh."

Oscar laughed. "Oh, they're nice. I only just started dating Roman, but they've been great."

"Really?" Leo felt a little less like an outsider now. "Good."

"Tapas!" Roman announced as a waiter emerged bearing plates of food. A general round of applause went around.

As always, the food broke the ice, and conversation struck up.

The usual question came up pretty quickly: "What do you do?"

"I'm a forensic photographer."

Roman caught his breath and looked over at Dustin, then back at Leo. "Ahhh. I see. You work together?"

Leo half-smiled. "Sometimes. His hours are more regular. I'm on-call a lot. I'm pretty new at the department, so they give me a lot of overnight shifts. And I try to squeeze those around class hours—I'm taking classes."

"Oh, neat." Josh was listening in. "What in?"

"Just the basic requirements this year. Nothing's been jumping out at me yet. I really liked the look of some of the basic business courses, but everything else is just high school all over again," Leo laughed.

Tyler grimaced. "Gross. I'm glad I never went for that."

"What about you? What do you do?"

Tyler just answered vaguely that he drove, and Josh said he ran a farm nearby. Roman was a pilot, and Oscar ran a dance studio.

"Huh. A mixed bunch."

"Wait 'til you hear the rest," Dustin laughed quietly. "We all pretty much started in the same place, and then…" He made a spreading motion with his fingers. "Kaboom. Went in all directions. Falcon's an artist, Blane's a vet—zoo," he quickly added with a significant smile. "Nico works for the park service, and Deen's in music."

"That's…" It took Leo a second to wrap his brain around it all. "Wow. That's cool." No wonder Dustin had seemed so open-minded about his career history and current trajectory. "No boring jobs here."

"I'm probably the most boring one." Dustin laughed. He didn't seem as shy as he usually did in large groups, like at the office party. It made Leo glad to see.

"No," Leo said quickly, glancing over at him. "Without you, my work would be useless."

Dustin looked pleased as he glanced down and popped another piece of crusty bread in his mouth. He modestly shrugged.

"Finally, someone who appreciates him." Roman elbowed Leo and clapped his back.

"Oh, of course. Though it sounds like you guys have his back, too." Leo smiled back at him. It felt like a test of some kind.

"I am right here," Dustin pointed out, and they laughed.

The conversation shifted to people's days at work and catching up on inside conversations, with frequent breaks to discuss how boring Josh and Tyler were for their stunt and their lacking love lives.

The humor never stopped, and only when the canvases were brought out did Leo realize his cheeks were hurting from smiling.

Dustin was right. They get me. Leo had always believed you could tell a lot about someone from his friends, and these guys all seemed cool. Maybe this was going to work out perfectly.

"And now, you're going to paint something for your date!"

Aw, shit. No sooner did I think that...

Leo groaned and leaned around his canvas to see Dustin. "I apologize in advance. You don't have to put this up anywhere. We can burn it in a bonfire."

"How do you think I feel? I'm dating a damn artist," Blane complained. "I'm going pure modernism. Splotches all over for me."

"Just like some of us later," Deen muttered, not too quietly, prompting an outbreak of laughter and sexual jokes.

Leo picked up his brush and shook his head as he stared down the blank canvas. He was in too far now to back out.

CHAPTER
Nineteen

DUSTIN

"AND HOW LONG HAVE YOU BEEN HIDING THIS SWEETHEART from us?"

Dustin's cheeks flushed as Oscar leaned into him and topped up his glass of sangria. He glanced over at Leo, who was talking some kind of sports with Tyler.

"Hm?" Oscar prompted.

"Um. He—he is sweet, yeah."

"Completely sweet on you." Oscar grinned. "How long, then?"

Dustin cleared his throat. "Uh, not long. We don't really know—it's that awkward in-between stage."

"Not one night, but no rings ding-a-linging in the future?" Oscar clicked his tongue sympathetically. "He seems worth it."

"So everyone says," Dustin chuckled. "But I think everyone in my life is conspiring to get me hitched. Like I can't be perfectly happy like I am."

Oscar clicked his tongue again, his arm still around Dustin's shoulders. "I can see that. These guys mean well, but... well, we can all be a little pushy sometimes. When we see a couple guys who are *clearly* wonderful together..."

"You think?" Dustin grinned.

"The way you were teasing each other about your paintings? Come on."

Dustin's grin only widened. Leo's painting was hardly sophisticated, but it was a clearly recognizable attempt to paint the very same landscape photo that Dustin had given him, and now sat on his desk.

For his part, Dustin had painted a bar that looked very much like the bar where they'd bumped into each other. The people sitting at it were creative interpretations of what humans looked like, but Leo had definitely recognized it, too.

And, most importantly, they'd had fun all night. Taking some time to be together in public without the inevitable ramping up of sexual tension that happened every time they were alone was surprisingly nice.

Surprisingly romantic, Dustin had to admit he really meant.

"Yeah," he finally said, chuckling and patting Oscar's back as he finished his glass of sangria and shook his head. "That's it for me. I've got to make sure we get an Uber back to an address somewhat near one of ours."

"Valentine's night stretches ahead of us like my legs..."

"Wide-open?" Dustin guessed.

Oscar grinned. "And going on and on." He pirouetted away and winked.

It was surprisingly sweet to walk up to Leo and have Leo's hand automatically rest on his back as he kept on talking about some farm thing with Tyler and Josh.

"Don't let us bore you," Tyler said after a minute. "We're just talking about machinery."

"Boys and their toys," Dustin chuckled.

"Speaking of your boy toys," Tyler said to Leo. "We should let you guys all get going. Everyone else has a nice, wholesome night ahead, I'm sure."

"And you two are joining the priesthood?" Leo raised a brow.

Josh snickered. "I doubt that," he drawled. "Lots of pretty boys on the town tonight."

For once, Dustin wasn't going to be one of them. He'd tried pointedly avoiding the scene so he didn't have to think about being alone the next morning. He'd also tried going out to make the most of the night. Neither had made him particularly happy.

This, though? Dinner and drinks and fun with his friends?

This was totally different. It made him glow inside with a kind of satisfaction he hadn't even known existed.

"We should get going, though," Leo agreed. "It being a work night and all." He poked Dustin in the chest. "For some of us responsible kids."

They shrugged on their jackets, their goodbyes taking longer than the greetings had. All the guys seemed to like Leo. Just as he'd said—and hoped fervently was true.

"Friday, right? Coming out for drinks?" Blane caught him before he left. "Both of you."

Leo looked startled and glanced at Dustin for guidance.

"Well, if you're not at work—" Dustin said. He wasn't going to stop them if they wanted to make Leo feel welcome among them.

Leo shook his head. "On-call that afternoon. Not that night."

"Perfect!" Blane grinned.

"See you then," Leo smiled. He waved to everyone, then escorted Dustin outside on his arm.

It feels kind of like he's my boyfriend already. Dustin tried not to look behind himself, knowing they would tease the hell out of him if they could. Instead he clung to Leo, his heart racing. "Share an Uber?"

"I should hope so," Leo smiled. "Unless the date went that terribly."

"No. Not at all," Dustin murmured. He glanced around at the clear sidewalk, then stretched onto his toes to steal a quick kiss. "It was perfect."

"I had a lot of fun," Leo said, his voice as quiet as Dustin's. It felt like they were magnetically drawn toward each other, a trance settling around them in the surprisingly quiet evening.

Dustin's shoulder rested against Leo's chest before he knew it, Leo's arms around his waist.

Hell, in the middle of the Knoxville gay district, he still wasn't used to this. And it had to be brand-new for Leo. But that newness gave Leo a kind of confidence—a certainty that he was entitled to cuddle in public—that Dustin drew on.

"Mmm," Dustin hummed after a minute. "How much longer?"

"A minute away."

Dustin pulled back reluctantly and took Leo's hand. "Thank you for coming out with me tonight. Do you have the Uber going to my place or yours?"

"Yours… to drop you off, if you wanted," Leo told him. "I

didn't want to assume." The more of a chance he gave Leo to break his heart, the more careful Leo seemed to be with it.

Dustin pressed another quick kiss against his cheek. "In that case, come in."

They barely made it through the cab ride without PDA. Just holding hands in the darkness made Dustin's heart race with anticipation—especially the way Leo's thumb gently rubbed along the side of his hand, his broad hand engulfing Dustin's.

It was all too easy to imagine what was about to happen. By the time they actually got to his house, his body was crackling with desire.

However much he said he wanted romance, he couldn't seem to keep his hands off Leo. Every goddamn time he had the chance, he threw himself at him. But hey, he figured. If that broke the spell between them, so be it. Life was short, and the sex was great.

"I love the way you smile," Leo murmured as he unlocked the door.

Dustin blinked, taken aback by the sudden comment. He caught himself smiling in response, his cheeks round and warm. "Oh."

"Yeah. Like that. When you were with your brothers, it was so… natural and relaxed. Not at all like you at work."

They kicked their shoes off and unzipped each other's jackets playfully.

"Oh, I know." Dustin pushed the jacket off Leo's shoulders. "I feel… safe around them, I guess."

That was it. He stopped in his tracks, the jacket not quite over his hands.

Leo took over and shook it the rest of the way off, then slid his arms around Dustin's waist. "What?"

I feel safe around him. Holding Leo, or being held by him, felt like… he could say anything and Leo would just smile and hold him tighter.

Dustin let his breath out and pressed his forehead to Leo's shoulder. "I like the fairytale stuff. The… gushy stuff. You know? Like tonight. Dates."

"Real dates. More of them are in our future," Leo promised quietly. "I like seeing you happy. If that makes you happy, we'll do it."

Dustin swallowed back the emotion in his throat. "I'm not used to…"

"Getting what you ask for? What you deserve?"

Dustin managed a quick nod. No way was he going to cry now and ruin the mood, but Leo was rocking him anyway as they hugged, swaying gently back and forth. "I sensed that," Leo murmured. "Never be afraid to ask, baby. If it's in my power, I'll do it."

"Why?" Dustin pulled back slowly until he was sure he had himself under control, taking his hand. They walked slowly to the living room, bypassing the bedroom for now.

"Why do I want to spoil you?" Leo asked, as if to clarify. When Dustin nodded, he chuckled. "Because I can. Because… life is way too fucking short to be an asshole. Especially to people you love, but to anyone at all, really."

"Is that a military thing?" Dustin settled in Leo's lap when they sat, pressing his shoulder against Leo's chest.

"Partly," Leo murmured, his arms sliding around Dustin's waist. "Part of it is the way I grew up. Respecting people, you know?"

Dustin nodded. Southern manners—even in a verbal disagreement—were real.

"Part of it is just wanting to grab what I have," and Leo's

arms tightened playfully around Dustin's waist, "and hold tight. Because I've never been this lucky before."

"Never gotten lucky this much?" Dustin teased to lighten the mood, walking his fingers up Leo's side.

Leo grimaced like he was admitting something personal, then nodded. "I hope it's not bad..."

"What? No," Dustin shook his head firmly. "You're perfect. I mean—no human is perfect, but..." Leo was laughing. "What?"

Leo tried to straighten his face. "There's your practicality again. Even though you want a fairy tale, you're... grounded. I love that about you."

Someone loves that about me? Dustin was almost speechless for a moment. "It's... a contradiction, I know."

"There's no shame in wanting more. As long as you don't screw yourself out of a good thing when you have it," Leo murmured.

"I try not to," Dustin chuckled. He drew a quick breath and then added, "But I'd like to screw myself into a good thing tonight."

Leo's hands slid under Dustin's shirt, up his back. "Oh, really?"

The warm, firm touch sliding up his back to his shoulder blades was incredibly distracting, and Dustin struggled to find words for a second. "I—yes." He wasn't sure if he was agreeing, or begging for more of Leo's skillful touches.

"That sounds like a perfect way to finish the night." Leo's hands were suddenly busy tugging his sweater off, leaving him in his shirt and tie. Then, Leo loosened Dustin's tie and unbuttoned his shirt slowly.

Dustin leaned into the touch, closing his eyes and letting Leo take over. Just for a minute. Just for now.

Leo pushed his shirt open, then tickled his stomach with the end of his tie. When Dustin squirmed, his eyes flying open as he whimpered his protest, Leo laughed. "Sorry. Couldn't resist."

Dustin rolled his eyes and tugged his tie and shirt off, tossing it all aside. "There."

"Oh. I like that much better." Leo's hands slid from his waist up to his back and down his arms, then up his front as he explored. Again, Dustin let him, just reveling in the touch for a minute. "Are you going to let me have you tonight?"

"You can have whatever you want," Dustin whispered, and he meant it. Every goddamn thing they'd done together had left him breathless with ecstasy.

"What do *you* want?" Leo paused, his hands cupping Dustin's cheeks. When Dustin opened his eyes, Leo pressed a gentle kiss to his lips.

The attention flustered Dustin for a moment. He closed his eyes again, drawing a breath as he tried to think. "Other than your cock in me?"

Leo moaned his agreement and pulled Dustin's hips against his until their hard cocks bumped and slid together. "And?"

"You… just…" Dustin trailed off, trying to think of a phrase other than *making love*. "Making me feel…" Leo wasn't saying anything, giving him a chance to finish. Damn it. "Important."

"You are," Leo whispered, pressing kisses against Dustin's neck now. "To a lot of people."

Dustin squirmed again with embarrassment. The sudden outpouring of words was exactly what he wanted, but it was out of the blue. He couldn't resist asking, "You really like me?"

"Have I not been obvious enough?" Leo grinned, tickling Dustin's stomach again to get him to open his eyes. When Dustin did, he pecked his lips again and chucked his chin with two fingers to keep him looking at him. "I do," he said firmly when Dustin wasn't looking away.

Dustin swallowed at the honesty he saw on Leo's face. He couldn't help but believe him.

"I thought… I don't know. That this was all so new for you," Dustin murmured. "Or that you just wanted to try out the sex."

"I love the sex," Leo grinned. "But it's *you* I want."

The words sank in, leaving indelible marks in his mind. There was no way in hell he was ever going to forget them.

Dustin grabbed Leo's cheeks and kissed him hard.

Leo sharply moaned in surprise, then again in arousal, grinding against him again. "Mixed messages," Leo managed when Dustin let him get some breath.

"Stop talking." Dustin laughed with Leo, then kissed him again. This time he nipped Leo's lower lip, sucking gently on it before letting go and pressing open-mouthed kisses against his mouth.

They were panting into each other's mouths by the time Dustin had Leo's shirt unbuttoned and pushed at the arms to indicate that Leo could get it off.

"Let's take this to my room," Dustin directed.

Leo mimed zipped lips and winked.

"Are you complaining about the messages?" Dustin grinned. "Either of them?"

"If I'm reading them both correctly—no," Leo smiled back. He rose to his feet, then hoisted Dustin into his arms and spun him around once as he kissed him again.

Dustin laughed, clinging to Leo. Being in his strong arms

didn't give him pause for even a moment. He trusted him to hold on tight.

I love this. I love him. I... fuck. I love him. I never meant to fall for him so fast. Dustin drew a quick breath, then batted Leo's shoulder. "Bed. Now." He needed to think about something else, fast.

Leo winked. "Oh, yes, sir."

They stumbled into his bedroom together, still kissing with every step, hands running over each other's torsos.

Leo's hands slid into his jeans, cupping his ass and squeezing gently. "God," Leo moaned against his mouth. "Speaking of a couple handfuls."

Dustin had almost forgotten that moment from earlier that night. He laughed, and while he tipped his head back to do so, Leo leaned in and kissed his throat. The laugh turned into a moan of approval and pleasure. Those lips sought the sensitive spots on his throat and neck, beelining between them.

"Fucking..." Dustin trailed off, digging his nails into Leo's shoulders. "Oh!" Leo was kissing behind his ear now, then nibbling his earlobe. "Fuck!"

"I take it you approve," Leo murmured huskily into his ear. "You can always ask me to ravish you. It's my pleasure."

Dustin's head spun with adrenaline when he was pushed backward and lost his balance. He hit the bed and gasped, already fighting his jeans off. He didn't want those in the way any longer.

Leo laughed gently, leaning down to kiss him again.

Dustin stopped halfway through pushing his own jeans over his thighs to watch Leo's hands at work, his jaw dropping.

The casual way he unbuttoned his trousers and pushed

them down, hooked his underwear with a thumb and dragged that down, too…

And Leo's cock sprang free, standing thick and proud and *hard* just inches away. What else was Dustin gonna do but suck it?

"You and me, we're getting tested next week," Dustin informed Leo, his eyes on that thick shaft. "I'll make an appointment."

Leo grinned and held his hands up in agreement. "Well, if you insist. Yes, sir."

"Good." Dustin winked, rolling onto his belly and propping himself up on an elbow as he kissed the shaft from base to tip. "If you don't mind…"

"I don't mind," Leo said, sounding breathless. "Whatever you want to do, baby. I'm all yours."

"Good. I want to taste you," Dustin whispered, gazing up past the thick cock head to meet Leo's eyes.

Leo's mouth hung open, his eyes fixed on Dustin like he was the center of the world. "Yes. Suck me, babe."

Dustin wrapped his hand around the shaft and slid it down to the base to hold Leo steady, and then he sucked the head into his mouth. With one smooth slide, his lips met his curled forefingers and he angled his head so he could take him into his throat.

"Your mouth feels fucking… Jesus. So good!" Leo moaned, his trousers dropping as he pushed them out of the way, then grabbed Dustin's shoulders. "Oh, fuck."

Dustin moaned around the mouthful, enjoying the velvety slide of bare skin across his tongue as he pulled his head up, lapping at the head. With each bob of his head, Leo grew harder and thicker in his mouth until he was fully erect and so ready for him.

Dustin let him have an extra minute of pleasure just to himself while he finished working his own pants off one-handed, wrapping his hand around Leo's hip and pulling it close.

"Can I?" Leo whispered, gently pushing with his hips when he was directed.

Dustin closed his eyes and breathed the scent of him as his shaft slid over his lips. "Mmhmm."

Leo was gentle as he moved his hips slowly, experimentally. "Oh. Fuck. Oh, my god. You have no idea how good your mouth is," he whispered. "One of these days, I wanna come all over your tongue, straight down that talented throat of yours… but I'll save that for another time, hm?"

Dustin shivered with arousal. It took all his self-control not to suck harder and tempt Leo to the edge. He *did* want Leo inside him tonight, after all.

He slowly pulled his head back when Leo slid out of him. "If you insist," he teased.

Leo grinned wolfishly. "Oh, yes. I want your legs over my shoulders now, baby."

"Oooh." Dustin loved that idea. He fought the last of his clothing off, then flopped on his back.

Leo crawled over him, pushing his legs up to his ears just as he'd promised. "Let me know if I hurt you."

"You're fine," Dustin assured him with a grin.

When Leo's slick fingers pressed against him, he finally relaxed and closed his eyes, stretching his arms above his head and letting Leo take charge of him.

It was so damn *good* to just let go and let Leo pleasure him —and Leo did just that, his fingers finding Dustin's prostate and rubbing in maddeningly gentle circles, then firmer.

He was throbbing with arousal and the need for something thicker than fingers within minutes. "Fuck. Hurry the fuck up and fuck me."

"Who's romantic now?" Leo teased.

Dustin burst out laughing, even though his legs were pressed against his chest, his heels by his hips. It should have been a vulnerable moment, but even now, Leo was making him laugh. *One good reason I love him.*

"I'll fuck you romantically, though," Leo added with a warm smile, leaning down to kiss him. "Nice and slow…" He eased his fingers out, and his cock pressed against Dustin a moment later. "And gentle, and then harder…"

Dustin moaned and pressed against Leo, but his range of motion was so damn limited. As Leo slid his knees over his shoulders, it was even more so, leaving him waiting for the mercy of that thick cock sliding into him.

"And then I'll make the mattress squeak with how hard I fuck you, until you're quivering on the edge. And I'll kiss you and tell you how fucking beautiful you are."

Dustin breathed out hard as the words hit him, and the thick shaft pressed inside, slowly.

"That's it," Leo whispered. "Oh, you're beautiful. Are your legs okay?"

Dustin managed a quick nod, his breathing deep and deliberately even. The pain faded to sparks of pleasure, and then tingles that started quivering deep in his stomach.

There it was. He was ready.

"Come on," he whispered.

Just as he promised, Leo went slowly at first, his palm on Dustin's cheek. With Dustin's legs there, he couldn't quite kiss him through it all, except by bending Dustin in two for a few brief moments.

It was almost more intimate when Dustin couldn't close

his eyes and disappear into a kiss. Now he could only watch, unable to break eye contact as Leo watched every expression of pleasure flicker over his face.

"Yes," Dustin whimpered, his hands curling into fists as he grabbed the sheets. "Oh, fuck."

Their bodies moved together as one, breathing coming in harsh pants against each other's cheeks as Leo pushed into him in quicker, harder thrusts.

Exactly as he'd promised, the mattress was squeaking within minutes and Dustin's nails were digging into the fabric of his bedspread as he cried his pleasure with every thrust.

"You're so gorgeous under me," Leo murmured between moans. "I want to feel you squeezing that tight little ass around me forever. Your cock's so hard, too… move your leg a little… there."

His hand closed around Dustin's cock, and Dustin almost saw stars. "Fuck!" Dustin cried.

"Sorry." Leo's grip softened a little as he laughed. "I just want to jerk you off hard and fast, all the time. When you're on the edge of coming… I want to do filthy things to you all night long."

Dustin clenched hard around Leo, then grabbed his back and hauled him close enough for a kiss. He felt the strain in his muscles, but he didn't care. He was already tight with ecstatic tension, his body quivering on the edge of orgasm.

"Come on, baby," Leo whispered, his strokes hard and fast as his cock pounded into him. "Come for me. I love watching you come. Let yourself go. I've got you."

Dustin couldn't stop himself. His back arched, his head rolling against the pillow as he gasped Leo's name.

"I've got you, baby." Leo's whisper was for his ears only,

his grip just perfectly firm around Dustin's pulsing cock. "That's it. You're incredible…"

All Dustin could do was moan in response, his legs sliding off Leo's shoulders as Leo pulled out of him.

Leo tossed the condom aside and stroked himself hard and fast.

"Come on," Dustin echoed when he could manage words again. His eyes swept from the hard shaft to Leo's face. "Come for me, baby. Come *on* me. Show me I'm yours."

Leo's back arched and then he came almost silently, his expression sheer bliss.

Wet, sticky, and utterly happy, Dustin wrapped his arms around Leo's back and pulled him down against him.

They crashed together, both laughing, passion smeared between them.

"Was that what you wanted?" Leo whispered, his hand resting on Dustin's side as he stroked his ribs with a thumb.

Dustin could only put so much emphasis into his, "Yes."

Apparently, it was enough, though, because Leo laughed gently. "Good."

Fuck. I do love him.

Maybe real love didn't start with a fairytale; maybe it ended with one.

Hell, maybe this was lust and not love talking. Dustin didn't care. Wherever this was going, he was overthinking things. He had to learn to trust Leo as much as he did in these instinct-led moments. And he couldn't do that until he gave him a chance, as he had now.

So… if Leo wanted to date him, that seemed entirely reasonable.

He just had to ask for what he wanted.

Maybe on Friday night.

CHAPTER

Twenty

LEO

"I can't believe I even finished that paper on time," Leo groaned as Josh pushed a beer into his hand. "Well, *on time* when you take the extension into consideration."

"It doesn't sound like you're super-into these classes, you know, man." Roman spoke lightly, but he frowned. "Even if they are foundation classes."

Leo hesitated as he glanced around at the guys. For a moment, he wished Dustin were there to deflect, but he and Oscar had gone to grab a round of drinks. Going to the clinic was never fun—he and Dustin had damn well earned them.

"I haven't really connected with any of them. I'm kind of interested in business, but no other careers are jumping out at me. I just went back to school because they suggested it, really."

"You like photography." That was Falcon, his chin propped on his fist as he pushed his empty glass around. "Arts careers are tough."

"Tell me about it," Leo snorted. "And I'm not getting back into documentary work. At least, not the kind I did before."

A few of them exchanged looks, but they didn't pry, for which Leo was grateful.

"You want to keep using your photography skills, but in a different career field?"

"I've thought about going freelance." Leo nodded. "Not with a newspaper, though."

"Weddings?"

Leo made a face. "Being responsible for that one big day in people's lives? What if I screw it up?" He relished the idea of capturing love—the most intangible emotion, incredibly hard to show in a still image, yet the warmest and most intimately physical. It would be the furthest possible thing from what he'd done already.

Uh oh. That sounded like a challenge, and he was starting to get interested.

"You practice first. Engagement photos, proposal photos, photos of boyfriends wandering around meadows being cute…"

"I'm sure we could give you some chances to practice that," Blane offered with a big grin.

"Oscar would die if you guys got engagement photos," Roman laughed. "And then he'd want some."

"Engagement, or photos?"

"Probably both," Roman said, tapping his nose conspiratorially.

"Are all of you… out to your friends and family? Be a hell of a way to come out, sending them engagement photos." Leo laughed.

Deen grinned. "Surprise! It's a boy!"

Leo choked on the last sip of his beer, and Roman slapped his back.

"Sorry," Deen laughed.

"No, he isn't." Josh rolled his eyes. "But yeah, all of us are basically out by now. A couple assorted extended relatives probably don't know, but parents and friends and coworkers do, for the most part."

Leo nodded. "I was talking to Dustin about it. It sounds like all you guys figured it out pretty early."

It felt like everyone was holding their breath, even if they played it casually. "Yeah?"

"Well, what about if you... didn't?"

"Doesn't mean you're any less gay or bi than someone who did acknowledge it earlier," Blane said, glancing around as the others nodded. "And coming out sucks, but get used to it. It never ends."

Leo glanced over at the bar to see how much time he had before Dustin got back, and then frowned. It took him a second before he recognized the guy standing near him at the bar.

Victor.

"I'll be right back, guys." Leo had to scoot past the rest of them and make his way around the extra chairs they'd dragged to the edge of the booth. When he was finally in the clear, he strode quickly toward the bar, his mood darkening.

If he's being a dick, I'll kick his ass.

"Yeah, we were out on Valentine's. Sorry I stole your date," he heard Dustin say. His boyfriend sure looked unafraid as he collected beers in one hand.

The disgusted noise from Victor was predictable. "Are you *dating* him?"

Dustin hesitated for a second, then looked from the bottles he was gathering back to Victor coolly. "Yeah." His eyes slid to Leo over Victor's shoulder as he apparently noticed him, and then he tipped his chin up in a defiant gesture. "Why?"

Leo's chest felt warm. What was that—excitement? Yeah. He was happy that Dustin had said they were dating, even if it wasn't quite true. Or was it? True enough to tell Victor, anyway.

"I didn't know he was—"

"Hey." Leo let his back slap land solidly between Victor's shoulder blades to knock the wind out of him. "Fancy seeing you here."

Victor looked at him quickly, then scowled. "Of course you'd be here, with your..." He looked at Dustin.

When Leo followed his gaze, Dustin shook his head slightly at him. Leo hesitated, biting down the words that were about to spill out.

"Nice seeing you. Bye," Dustin said simply.

Victor snorted. "Really? This is a small fucking town, dude. You can't just *bye, Felicia* me."

"He can if he wants to," Leo said firmly.

Dustin cast him a glare. "Leo."

Leo shook his head slightly and looked away. It was impossible not to defend Dustin when Victor was deliberately winding them up, being as much of a dick as he could.

"You tell him, Dustin," Victor laughed.

"Leave us alone," Leo said, his voice harsher than he meant it to be. "We haven't done a thing to harm you. So you head on home now and leave us be."

Victor tipped his head left and right, but after he rolled his shoulders, he just strode off silently.

Dustin glared at him and shoved the beers back onto the counter. "I said, *no*."

"What?" Leo blinked at Dustin. "He's gone. That's what matters."

"It's not *all* that matters," Dustin muttered, running a hand over his hair. "It—no. You know what? Let's not do this. Let Oscar know I'm gone."

"Wh-What? I didn't mean—hold on," Leo said quickly, but Dustin was already pushing through the crowd for the door. He glanced between Dustin and the dozen beers on the counter. "Ah, shit."

Oscar joined him a minute later and frowned. "What did I miss?"

"Uh. I'm not sure," Leo admitted. He hadn't seen Dustin try anything this dramatic... well, ever. "He said to say he's gone."

"What did you *say?*" Oscar laughed, though his smile was cautious.

"It wasn't... well, it might have been me." Leo didn't understand yet. He grabbed half the beers and jerked his head toward the table.

They were all staring at him.

Someone asked, "What was that about?"

"Not sure." Leo grabbed his jacket. He didn't think it would look good to sit and drink with them while Dustin was upset. "I'll be back, maybe. See you around. Thanks for having me."

"Are you going after him?" Oscar asked.

"Of course I am," Leo snorted.

"Good. Let us know if we can do anything."

Leo took a moment to cast him an appreciative smile. "A translation sometime, maybe."

"Did he just pull an Oscar?" Falcon's brows rose. "Dramatics," he added for Leo's benefit.

"I… think so?" Leo zipped up his jacket and waved. "Anyway, see you next time. Hopefully." *If he doesn't dump me before we even really get together for saying something stupid.*

The goodbyes were swift, under the circumstances, but even so, by the time he got to the sidewalk, Dustin wasn't there.

"Goddamn it." He paced back and forth for a minute, but Dustin was nowhere within sight.

There was nothing else for it. He'd have to call him. Or maybe text—give him a chance to respond at his own pace, on his own terms. Given that all of this seemed to be about Leo storming in, calling might not be very sensitive.

Right. A text it was, then.

Leo called himself a cab first. If need be, he could ask them to change directions en route and head for Dustin's house. Then, once he was settled in the back seat, he pecked out a careful message.

Sorry I hurt you. Can we talk? I want to know what I screwed up. And your brothers will kill me if I don't make sure you're OK :)

Then, he followed up with another.

I'm on my way home but I can come over if you want. Just let me know.

The seconds ticked by. The road noise and the soft music playing in the background grew almost maddening as he waited for an answer, fidgeting and bouncing one foot over his crossed knee.

It felt like an eternity, even though it was only three minutes before he got a response.

We can talk but not tonight. Have to visit parents tomorrow. Sorry I left so fast. Are they mad?

"Oh, hon," Leo murmured and shook his head.

Of course they aren't, just worried like me. You're OK?

Dustin's response was much quicker now.

Yeah I'm OK. Thank you. xox.

Can we talk tomorrow? Leo asked.

If you come over before stupid family shit.

Do you want moral support during stupid family shit?

Dustin hesitated before answering. *Are you sure?*

Of course. It's stressing you the fuck out isn't it?

Yeah :(I'll explain more tomorrow if there's time.

I'll be over first thing, Leo promised.

Just... thank you.

Leo finally relaxed enough to breathe deeply. *Of course babe. Sleep well. xox.*

You too. Dustin included a kissing emoji at the end of the message, which, as far as Leo was concerned, meant he was forgiven.

With that much settled, though his heart was heavy, enough hope had crept back to let him sleep.

Eventually.

DUSTIN LAUGHED WHEN THE DOORBELL RANG. THE SUN WAS barely up, so that had to be Leo.

The man's commitment to keeping his word was… well, something he hadn't experienced before from someone who was interested in him *this* way.

Sure enough, Leo stood there—in a nice dress jacket, collared shirt, and sweater, no less. He looked every inch the boyfriend who was ready to be introduced to his parents.

"Hi," Dustin greeted, still laughing.

Leo looked confused for a moment, glancing down at himself and then at Dustin. "Did I forget my pants?"

No matter what the conversation that lay in wait for them, Dustin's spirits had already soared at just the sight of Leo. His mood and energy lately had been several times better than even a month ago, and he could trace the root cause: Leo.

Leo was doing wonders for him without even knowing it.

"It's… I can't believe you're here is all," Dustin told him, stepping aside to let him in and keep the heat in. Mid-

February wasn't the best weather to be chatting on the doorstep.

"Is it too early?" Leo looked him over, no doubt noticing that he was already dressed and up for the day, too.

"No, I've been up for a while," Dustin said. The part he didn't add was, *worrying about all this.*

"I don't think I slept great last night either," Leo said with a quick smile. He toed his shoes off and shrugged off his jacket.

Dustin took the jacket from him to hang it up. "I'm sorry if I worried you. I didn't mean to."

"I know. It's okay."

"Should we...?" Dustin jerked his chin toward the living room. This conversation wasn't really a front-hall conversation, either.

"Yeah." Leo took Dustin's hand, and Dustin let him. That seemed to relax the tension between them.

By the time they settled down, Dustin was tucked against Leo's side, Leo's arm around his shoulder.

Leo smiled at him. "I thought a lot about last night and I kind of... had a guess what I did wrong. But I want you to say what you want."

Dustin swallowed hard. "I'm bad at that."

"Asking for things? I've noticed." Leo rubbed his shoulder. "You might be quieter than the other guys, but you can stand up for yourself when you're with them. With me—you let me call the shots."

Dustin blew out a quick breath. Leo wasn't holding back, was he? "Yes and no. I don't stand up for myself among them enough, either. It's the same with my parents."

"You're tired of having everyone else fight your battles."

Dustin opened his mouth, and then closed it again and stared at Leo. *How can I improve on that?*

Leo chuckled at the look he was giving him. He shrugged. "It only makes sense."

"You're fucking smart," Dustin informed him. When Leo tried to shrug it off, he insisted, "No, you are."

"Nah. I care, that's all. I want to know what bothers you. And I want to make sure I don't do it again." Leo shook his head. "You did ask me not to get involved, and I still couldn't help myself, because *I* was annoyed. That was stupid of me."

It was Dustin's turn to shake his head. "No, I get it. He was winding you up as much as me."

"But I took the bait when you didn't." Leo rubbed Dustin's shoulder. "I need to learn that. I admire that."

Dustin stared. "Really?" He'd spend the night thinking he'd seemed like a coward to Leo, but... Leo was seeing it completely differently.

"Yeah. It makes sense as a strategy to avoid conflict—especially back in our high school days, and in the office when you have assholes like Victor around. We're all taught things like de-escalation, you know," Leo chuckled. "Of course I recognize it."

Dustin nodded dumbly. That was his own fault for assuming Leo was going to escalate the conflict, just because... what? He'd been in the military? No, that was his fear talking. "I just thought, if it got to a fight, I wouldn't be able to stand up for myself against Victor, who's trained in... you know. Fighting."

"Right..." Leo nodded slowly, not following him yet.

"And then you'd have to stand up for me..."

Leo's expression cleared up instantly. "Ah. Yeah. Babe, if I ever punch him, it's something *I* wanted to do," he told Dustin and grinned. "Believe me."

Dustin laughed quietly. "Yeah. The timing was just bad. With me realizing that the guys have been trying to shelter me since Bryce—that was my high school ex, who was all about the sex," he added.

"Bryce. I even hate his name," Leo grumbled.

A warm, affectionate glow burned in Dustin's chest as he watched Leo. Having him feel protective did actually feel nice, when he put his ego aside. "And then my parents wanting to set me up with some random asshole just because he's got money, *again*... I haven't been back for lunch in a couple weeks."

Leo ran his hand down Dustin's arm and back up slowly. "Like I said, if you want backup, I'm there."

Dustin swallowed hard. "I need to work on standing up for myself. Without just running away."

"You're safe with me," Leo promised quietly. "I should warn you now: I'll let you talk things out with them, but I won't let them be assholes to you."

Dustin let his breath escape in a long sigh and pressed his forehead against Leo's shoulder. "I'm ready to tell them to listen to me—and if they don't... I don't know. To walk away until they hear the message."

Leo squeezed him so tightly it felt like his shoulders were pressing together. "I know, baby. I'm proud of you."

"It would probably help if I have a good reason not to go on any more stupid dates," Dustin mumbled, before he could talk himself out of it. His heart was pounding. He couldn't see Leo's face, but he could feel the hitch in Leo's breathing.

"Well," Leo said slowly. "We could say we're dating. By many definitions, we are."

Ask for what you want, dumbass. Dustin's throat felt tight. "Are we?"

"What do *you* want?" Leo asked softly.

He's waiting for me to be ready. Dustin's foot jiggled against the floor as he pressed closer to Leo. "Would you… be my boyfriend?"

"I love you."

Or was that *I'd love to?*

Dustin's heart nearly stopped. Either way, the end result was the same, wasn't it? He wasn't about to ask for clarification and ruin the moment. But he certainly knew how he felt.

"You… do want to be?"

"Duh." Leo pulled away from him and grinned when Dustin looked at him. "That was way too easy."

Dustin tilted his head. "*Too* easy? Would you like some more struggle and strife first?"

Leo chuckled quietly, and Dustin knew he was onto something. "It's like I'm used to living on the edge. I am, I guess. I haven't had any one big, defining experience like you and that asshole Bryce, but… nothing has been this easy or…" He seemed to struggle for words.

"Good?" Dustin asked.

Leo thought about it, then nodded. "Yeah. *Real*, I think. Nothing's been this real."

Dustin ran his hand along Leo's leg and caught his hand. "I know."

"It's just going to take time," Leo murmured.

"Of course." Watching his friends find love had taught Dustin that it was never expected. It seemed to catch each of them by surprise. Hell, some of them had tried to hide it at first, not sure about what they were feeling—or sure, but not confident in their own feelings.

And he'd done exactly the same thing. Just because his heart wasn't governed by logical rules, and he couldn't test his feelings or put them under a microscope, didn't mean it wasn't worth listening to.

"I want you," Dustin said simply. "What will take time? Telling everyone? Is it the gay thing?"

Leo laughed. "*The gay thing*," he echoed. "Partly, I guess. But partly just… adjusting to having something good that I don't have to fight to keep. In fact, the more I try to, the worse it'll be. I learned that last night."

Dustin paused to think about it. Leo wanted to protect him—and that wasn't a bad thing. It actually made his heart soar to know that someone wanted to. "And I'm working on letting you hold on."

Leo laced their fingers. "Good. Because I'm not letting go. Now—when do we leave to see your parents?"

Oh, God. I don't know if I can do this. I have to get it out of the way with now.

"How about right now?"

Leo smiled, and in that smile Dustin found what he was looking for—not just compassion, but understanding. "Okay. Let's go."

Twenty-Two

LEO

"So, what do you do?"

Here it was: the question Leo had been braced for since they'd arrived at the house—not even three minutes ago.

Dustin cast him a significant look, and Leo just smiled calmly back at him. He wasn't going to stress his new boyfriend out any more. He felt much more pressure than he let on, but that was covered in his training, too.

"I'm a forensic photographer," Leo answered. "I'm the guy recording evidence before they bag it and send it to Dustin."

"Oh." Dustin's parents exchanged looks.

"What about you, Mr. Reed? Mrs. Reed?" Leo asked to distract them from their internal calculations.

"Oh, please. Joe and Eliza." It was an outwardly warm reception—Eliza was even serving tea. But Leo could sense the undercurrent of tension, from the way Dustin had briefly hugged both his parents. There was some elephant in the room. Either the one he knew about, or something else. "I took an early retirement option when my company merged…"

Joe went on an explanation of his company's merger while Leo listened politely and nodded.

His job was to try to defuse the tension, even though he had the feeling that would normally be Dustin's job. But Dustin was wound up to hell. He could sense it in the way Dustin walked stiffly and forced smiles.

"So, how long have you been, um... photographing things?"

"I've been in town for a few months now, sir," Leo answered. He couldn't go wrong with being too formal, he figured. "But I've been a photographer for a while. I started when I grew up here. Same school as Dustin—we didn't hang out in the same circles, but we sort of knew each other." He figured some history would work in his favor. "I left when I joined the military. Same career, more or less." No way was he answering an interrogation about that. "When I left, I wanted to see what home was like. There was a job open, so..." He shrugged. "It all kind of fell into place, like it was meant to be."

"Oh, I see. A military man." Joe straightened up with satisfaction and looked at Dustin. "We said Dustin should go for that route, you know."

Leo politely nodded.

"But he was determined to go his own way, weren't you?" Joe looked at Dustin. "Always has been."

"And now look at me." Dustin was drinking tea, but Leo had the impression he was doing so to try to stay silent.

"One of the best lab technicians in the county," Leo added. "Everyone says it."

Dustin looked startled as he glanced over. "Really?"

Leo gave him a warm smile. He'd had the feeling that

would brighten up Dustin's day—and endear him to his parents.

But Eliza was frowning. "The police are so underfunded, you know. All across the state."

Counting down to three...

"They can't be paying what those kinds of skills are worth. None of their new job openings have been anywhere close to fair," Joe picked up on her thread.

Not even three. One and a half. Leo forced a smile. "Oh, I can't complain. I've thought of retraining, but photography is my deepest skill set."

"That can be hard on a young couple. When we got together, we were both at the bottom of the pay scale." Joe sighed. "Things were easier in the private sector."

Leo's eyes glinted as he glanced at Dustin, who was looking steadily more annoyed. *Okay. I'll fix this one way or another.* "Oh, don't worry about us. The VA takes good care of me."

That put them in an awkward position—either they had to disagree that the VA did its job and sound unpatriotic, or worse, ungrateful for his service, or they agreed and thought he was being compensated adequately for his time.

They saw it, too. Joe's brows furrowed for a moment. Eliza opened her mouth and closed it again.

And then Dustin interjected, "But most important, I found a guy who makes me happy."

There. Done. Leo's chest swelled with pride at the way he and Dustin had defused the first meeting. Hopefully they weren't sticking around long enough to give his parents more chances to pry, though.

Eliza sighed. "Yes. Yes, I always did say that was important. Cookies, anyone?"

"That was… I can't believe it."

Dustin had barely made it to the car before turning to Leo, his expression alight.

Leo shook his head. "Me neither," he murmured. The intense focus on salaries so quickly? Not the most comfortable of in-law meetings.

"They gave up so easily. No more *meet this trust fund baby*," Dustin sighed.

"Wait, *easily*?" Leo's brows furrowed. "You had to bring home a goddamn boyfriend for them to stop setting you up with guys. They were throwing trust fund babies at you?"

"Well. Not literal babies. I'd almost prefer that," Dustin snorted. "Babies are cute, at least. Overgrown man-children who haven't had to work a day in their lives…"

Leo laughed and squeezed Dustin's hand, then reclaimed his hand so he could make a left turn. "Don't worry, honey. I promise there's no trust fund backing me up. On the other hand, there's no trust fund… and the VA *is* kind of screwing us all over these days. Underfunding everywhere. Your parents aren't totally wrong."

"Don't care," Dustin shook his head. "They were young and broke, too. They said it themselves. They figured it out. If things get bad, we'll find a way."

Leo let his breath out and nodded. *He really is an apple that fell far away from the tree. I'm so glad.* "I'm glad they respected me enough to back off. I just wish they respected you more in your own right."

"I…" Dustin trailed off. He rested a hand on top of Leo's on the shift. "Yeah. Me too. Everyone else has seen it before, too. I think it's oldest-child syndrome. They have to get everything perfectly right in my life—even though I moved out years ago."

"And they want things to be better for you than them," Leo agreed. "But that doesn't mean trying to run your life."

All of Dustin's issues speaking up about what he wanted made perfect sense now. His parents had a way of abruptly steering the conversation where they wanted, making things about what they wanted, so fast that Leo hadn't even been able to shut it down. All he could do was try to play their game.

"I should have told them to stop asking about money," Dustin mumbled. He wouldn't meet Leo's gaze when Leo looked over. "Sorry."

"It's not like I didn't have warning," Leo assured him. "It's fine. You don't have to shelter me. Your parents aren't monsters. But the more you learn to ask for what you want, the easier it'll be for you to stand up to them, too."

Dustin squeezed his hand. "I hope so. You seem so... confident in all of this. I mean, this has been a thing for *years*. You just played their game within ten minutes of meeting them."

"It's easier for me *because* it's less personal," Leo told him. "You're tied up in it. Of course it's hard, babe. You've had a lifetime of them talking over you."

Dustin was quiet for a few moments, rubbing Leo's hand gently. "Yeah. You're right. What about you?"

"What about me?" Leo's chest tightened. He had a feeling he knew what was coming.

"Your parents. Have you told them? It's a small enough city that word might get around if you don't."

He was completely right. Leo knew it. But that was the one thing he'd been putting aside—putting off for the future, a better time, when he was more settled and certain in his career, and…

Aw, hell. He was avoiding his own shit, too. If Dustin was confronting his demons, the least Leo could do was the same.

"I need time to figure out how to tell them," Leo admitted quietly. "I don't think it'll be bad. Just tense."

They were at Dustin's house already.

"Want me to come in?" Leo asked.

Dustin glanced at him, then crookedly smiled. "And get us both distracted?"

"Probably," Leo admitted with a laugh. "Or I could drop you off here, and then take you on a date next week… and let the anticipation build…"

Dustin shivered. "Yes. I mean, um. The date bit. I guess I should do the stuff I've been, uh… avoiding."

"Yeah," Leo grinned. The pile of homework on his desk at home said the same to him. "Look at us. Not even fucking like bunnies *every* spare minute."

"How grown-up," Dustin sighed.

"We don't have to be grown-up all the time," Leo assured Dustin and smiled. "Just sometimes."

Dustin leaned in to kiss him and smiled back. "Thank you. For… everything."

"Of course, babe." Leo unbuckled so he could squeeze Dustin in a tight hug. "Text your brothers, too, before they kill me."

Dustin laughed and pressed his lips against Leo's again in a slow, warm kiss. "Of course," he murmured when he finally pulled back. "Nobody's getting their hands on you but me… my boyfriend."

Leo grinned back at him. "That's right, boyfriend of mine.

Get that sexy ass inside before I forget about all my responsibilities."

"Fine," Dustin laughed and kissed him again. "See you soon."

"See you, hon."

Leo stayed to watch Dustin get inside safely, giving him one more wave when Dustin turned back to look at him.

As he finally drove home, he cursed that very pile of homework that had pulled him away.

Speaking of facing his problems, something had to be done. Whatever he'd said to Dustin's parents, all those pieces weren't going to fall into place on their own.

CHAPTER
Twenty~Three
DUSTIN

"Dustin? I need you in interview room three, please."

Every one of Dustin's red flags went up at once: the casual tone Ron was taking as he glanced into the lab, the presence of HR anywhere near the labs, and the immediate nature of the request.

This was not good, and all evidence pointed to the problem: the brand-new relationship. So new he hadn't told anyone else about it. As far as he was concerned, that was none of their business anyway. Many of his coworkers talked freely about their home lives, but Dustin had always kept to himself that way.

Dustin also saw no other choice but to agree to the request. "Sure," he answered after a moment, even though he felt dizzy as he rose to his feet and locked his computer.

Why couldn't it have been a busy day in the lab? He had no excuses not to go.

Slowly, he rounded the corner, trying not to focus on the way his cheeks burned. It would only make him blush more, like he was guilty of anything. And as far as he was concerned, he wasn't.

"Ah, thanks." Ron was waiting to escort him—no, *accompany* him—to the room.

Dustin felt eyes on him as they walked briskly through the office to the interview rooms, all the way on the other side of the place.

God fucking damn it. Why did this have to happen on Monday? Day one of his first work week with a real boyfriend? Right when he was enjoying things getting easier for them?

Ron was trying to chat about his weekend, and Dustin stuck to grunts and nods in response. Ron seemed to take it as normal for him, though, and kept trying all the way until the interview room.

Goddamn extroverts, too. Dustin was already cranky. Being talked at wasn't going to help matters.

As he dropped into the chair, he realized that that was exactly what he was up for. His boss, Glen, was there. Come to think of it, he was also Leo's boss.

Dustin held himself straight and proud as he sat opposite the empty chair next to Glen, clearly meant for Ron.

If I wasn't sure before, I am now. Now I get to answer questions about my orientation to a couple straight old guys. Welcome to gay life, Leo.

"Ah, Dustin. How are things?"

"Pretty good. As you probably know," Dustin answered with a vague smile.

"Well, uh." Ron shuffled his papers. "I did—we did hear some rumors we wanted to clear up."

"Rumors in a department this size. How surprising," Dustin answered, but he didn't give them a smile to ease the tension. He was pissed about being dragged in here like a damn suspect.

"Ha ha. Well. We've heard… that… there are some rules being broken here. Conflict of interest. That sort of thing."

"This will probably work better if you actually say what you're talking about," Dustin stated, folding his hands in his lap. "You mean you heard I'm dating a coworker."

"Ah." Glen cleared his throat and nodded. "That's what we mean, yes. Something about you and…?" He trailed off as if giving Dustin a chance to supply another name.

Right. Like I want to cover up with some random girl. Dustin gazed back at them. They could goddamn say it, if they wanted to treat this like a police interview.

"Leo," Ron finally supplied. "Glen, I believe he's your new hire—"

"Yeah. Yeah, Leo Sanderson." They both looked awkward and apologetic, not accusatory like he'd expected.

"Yes, he's my boyfriend," Dustin answered, now that they'd come out with it.

"Right. As you're aware, in the employee rules, relationships are discouraged. In this particular case, uh… there could be conflicts of interest."

"What sort of conflicts?" Dustin asked mildly.

"Well… say you're working a case that he also worked. The defense lawyer could argue that you two were conspiring to, I don't know, frame the defendant, or protect each other if one of you made a mistake."

"As opposed to what they argue every damn time about us trying to cover for each other." Dustin smiled. "That's unheard-of, I'm sure."

Ron laughed awkwardly and looked at Glen.

"I don't have a problem with the two of you boys…" Glen

made an awkward gesture with a hand to the empty chair next to Dustin.

"Why call me in for a meeting alone, then? If you're worried about the two of us dating?" Dustin asked, raising his brows and looking between them.

"Well, er... we weren't sure about these rumors. Never like to get involved too early. Make accusations, that sort of thing. You understand. Your good name is worth a lot."

"My good name being tarnished by... being seduced by the new guy?" Dustin asked drily.

"Oh, no, no. Just—you see how it is," Glen stuttered.

Dustin propped his chin on his fist, folding his other arm across his chest to support it. "I'm afraid I don't. I can understand the conflict of interest argument—if a case comes up that affects either of us, we'll be sure to avoid it. Just like any best friends or spouses already in the department." He didn't pay much attention, but he was positive they couldn't be the only ones dating here.

"Right. Well, it could also be a... a screen for other motives," Ron said.

Dustin snorted. "Sure. Like homophobia. Where is this suddenly coming from?"

The other two looked at each other for a moment as if deciding whether they should share any more information.

His heart was still racing, but Dustin wasn't going to back down. In this new, improved era of Dustin, he was standing up for himself, and he wasn't going to worry about treading on toes when he was being wronged.

Without Leo there to back him up, he had to stand up for them both by himself. He wasn't going to let Leo down.

"It's not actually in the rules that it's not allowed, is it?" Dustin pressed.

"Well, there's supposed to be a notification… to your supervisors," Ron said faintly. Clearly, this wasn't going like he'd envisioned.

"Oh, I should have called on Saturday afternoon. Right after calling our best friends to let them know the good news," Dustin said drily. "This came up pretty damn fast."

"Saturday," Glen murmured to Ron as if it were significant, and Ron waved him off.

"The point is, kid…"

"I've been working here for five years," Dustin reminded him. "And you know I'm good at my job. Leo's damn good at what he does, too. He's watertight in court. He's appeared a few times, hasn't he?"

"It's true, but… how the thing looks, is all," Ron said weakly.

"Someone in the department doesn't want to be associated with the gays in forensics?" Dustin guessed. "Or someone thinks it's inappropriate in a public line of employment? If there's an actual complaint, I'd like to know about it."

"Not a complaint, exactly." Ron rose to his feet. "I see there's—things are already established…"

"I'm not dumping him because someone heard we were dating, if that's what you mean," Dustin laughed. "It's a lab, not a closet." Even Glen had to smile at that. "But I'd like to know who the hell is saying this is a problem all of a sudden. I mean, if you've hauled half of any other new couples into the office for disciplinary action before, I certainly haven't heard about it."

"Oh, this isn't disciplinary," Ron hastened to assure him. "Those protocols are—no, no. Certainly not."

"I don't think this is going anywhere productive," Glen

said with a smile, rising to his feet. "How about we let Dustin get back to his important work while we review employee policies?"

Dustin felt for a moment like Glen was on his side, but for all he knew, he was just trying to escape the incredibly awkward atmosphere in that room.

As he walked back to the lab, his hands shook around his phone. It took effort to compose a text without any extra letters.

They just pulled me into the office to say relationship might not be OK. I pointed out I've never heard of this rule.

Leo's response was quick.

WTF? How did they even know?

That's what I'm wondering.

There was a pause, and then Leo responded again with just one word.

Victor.

Twenty-Four

LEO

It wasn't hard to find the man he was looking for. One call to a coworker later, Leo heard that Victor and his partner, Kyle, were on-scene at another break-and-enter.

Better—or perhaps worse—it was just in the next neighborhood over from his own house. The break-ins had been steadily migrating in his direction, which was worrying.

"Hey. Forgot your gear?" Victor grinned. He was leaning against his car with a cup of coffee, standing behind the tape line.

Leo was in his running gear, a clingy t-shirt and track pants. He had made it look casual, almost accidental, that he'd run into them. Paul—the other forensic photographer—had his back. He wouldn't ask questions about why Leo wanted to know where Victor was.

"Yeah, I'll cut the bullshit. Did you snitch?"

Victor looked confused for a moment, looking at Leo and then around. "On what?"

"Me and Dustin." Leo had only gotten revved up by the jog over here, not calmed down like he'd hoped.

"Me? Tell? What do you mean?"

"HR," Leo sighed, leaning on the car next to Victor. The tape line between them was a thin damn barrier, but it was enough of one that it gave him extra boldness. "Look, man. Don't bullshit me. If you got a problem, tell me to my face."

"Does your boyfriend know we're talking?" Victor raised his brow. It sounded like it was intended as an insult.

"No. Why does that matter to you?"

"It doesn't. I didn't think he wanted you talking to me," Victor grinned.

Leo chuckled. "Nice avoidance. I take it that's a yes. Well, man. I've got a meeting with HR in an hour to *review my suitability for the position.*"

The surprise that crossed Victor's face was genuine. "What?"

"Yeah. Your little stunt might leave me out of a job. And if I am, I will have nothing better to do than stalk your ass for photographic proof of whatever fucking shit I can nail you with."

For the first time, Victor looked worried. "What?" he said again, his brows furrowed. "Man. I didn't tell on you. I think it's weird, all of that gay stuff," he gestured with his coffee cup. "And you going gay on me and not telling me…"

"I'm not gay. I'm bi. Remember, the question you didn't ask?"

Victor stared, then groaned. "God. Technicalities."

"Yeah, but an important one," Leo waved his hand. "Less important than my job right now, though. I don't believe you."

"I didn't," Victor protested. "Okay, I was pissed that you lied to me—"

"No lies, man. I'm not gay. I wasn't dating him then,

either. I'm bi, and now I am. If you'd just been able to spit it out—are you dating Dustin?—I would have told you." Leo sighed. "Look, I think we're just… different now."

"Right about that," Victor muttered and finished his coffee, waving his empty cup for a moment. "Damn. But I wouldn't try to get you fired. That's just below the belt."

That was a weird moral line in the sand if he was willing to harass Dustin at the bar, but whatever. "Are you sure?" Leo looked him dead in the eye, looking for any sign of dishonesty, but he found none.

Victor shook his head. "I'm sure. Maybe I'm kind of a dick, but I won't screw with a buddy's job."

Leo pinched the bridge of his nose and shook his head. Victor was the easy answer. If it wasn't him, there weren't many possibilities left for who could have reported them, and he didn't like any of them. "Okay, man. Thanks for being straight-up with me."

Victor hesitated, looking at his cup for a second, then threw out there, "I might know who did it. If you can't find out, let me know."

The weird gesture of friendship came out of the blue. Leo stared at him for a few moments, then shook his head. "Why?"

Victor waved a hand. "We were buddies once. Maybe I never liked Dustin, but I liked you. If you get fired, and I had something to do with it…" he trailed off, frowning. "That's not cool."

"But you said—"

"I didn't tell HR. But I might know who did. That's all I'm saying," Victor said firmly. "Just… see what you dig up."

What a day. Leo shook his head. "Okay, fine. I better head to my meeting. See you around, man."

The jog back home didn't turn up any magical answers. He showered and changed into something more professional, then grabbed his keys and headed for the office.

Before he left, he doubled back to grab his wallet. If he got fired, he was buying himself donuts on the way home.

"Hey, Josh? What's up?"

"Oh, hey! Leo. Not much, you?" Josh sounded worried. "Is everything okay?"

"Not sure yet," Leo admitted. Now he was glad he'd gotten Josh's number after their chat about machinery to send him some Wikipedia pages on modern armor. "You're the only one of Dustin's friends whose numbers I've got."

"Oh! Yeah. How can I be of service?" Josh chuckled.

Leo could hear what sounded like a horse neighing in the background. "Sorry, this a bad time?"

"No, no. Shoot."

"Well… I might need some of that photography work sooner than I thought. Also, I'm dating Dustin for real now."

"Uh… Shit. And congratulations. In that order… probably. Good luck with him," Josh joked.

Leo managed to crack a smile. He was leaning back in the driver's seat of his car, his car tucked in at the far end of the parking lot. He'd shown up early for the meeting, and hell if he was gonna walk in early and sweat it out inside. "Thanks."

"It's great to see you two together, for real," Josh added. "So, the photography work? You quitting?"

"Or being made to. I don't know. There's vague rules on dating coworkers… I don't think they usually apply them, but they might now, of course."

"Because of the gay," Josh said sarcastically. "Great. Man, you need to talk to Roman."

"Roman? Why? He a lawyer?"

"Pilot, but he got into some trouble over something else with HR a while back. Homophobic coworker. He knows Tennessee law a bit now. Hell, you've got boyfriend status," Josh drawled, "I'll add you to the group chat."

"Group chat? Thanks, I think." Leo rubbed his forehead with his arm as he stared down the building. He'd walked into war zones. He could do this.

"Does Dustin know yet?"

"Not sure if he knows how bad it is yet," Leo said. "But I'll catch him before I leave."

"Okay. We got your back, man. You should be in the chat now."

Leo's phone pinged, and he glanced down at the alert, then opened the thread. "Looks like it."

Roman sent a quick text: *Welcome, Leo! Leaving for work in 10. I hear I'm needed? I like to be needed. This is Roman.*

Leo laughed to himself. "Okay, I've got Roman's number. Thanks."

"Anytime, man."

He hung up and scrolled through the chat to answer. *Hey guys. Going into a work meeting in 5. Josh said you might know laws on being fired for excessive gayness.*

Oh hell no. Still illegal here, man. They can get you for something else though.

That's what I thought. Leo chewed his lip. *I'm on probation, so...*

Someone else—Falcon. *WTF? Because of you and Dustin? And does this mean you're dating???*

OMG, Oscar chimed in.

Beside the point, guys. Gimme a sec, Roman texted, followed by another message. *So 1) ask them why they're firing you, 2) get as much in writing, 3) don't you want to quit anyway?*

I did ask Josh if you guys have any of those sweet jobs lined up for me. Leo smiled to himself as his stress started to fade. Roman was right—this was a chance to make a leap. Whether or not they fired him, if they made it clear they didn't want couples working together, he could solve that for them.

He'd planned to do it over a bit longer a period of time, but when life handed you lemons…

OK, walking in now. TTYS.

Leo instantly got several good luck messages back, and his spirits lifted as he put a name to the new feeling. It was like he'd finally found somewhere he belonged: a chosen family, who took him exactly as he was and tried to help, even though they hardly knew him. Dustin had great taste in friends, if not in bosses.

Leo locked the car and strode to the building without fear. No matter the outcome of this meeting, his future was in his own hands—nobody else's.

And maybe the hands of a few new friends.

CHAPTER
Twenty~Five

DUSTIN

"Hey, Ron."

Dustin was leaning against the cubicle near interview room two, sipping his mug of coffee as he drew his lunch break out.

They'd been in there for twenty minutes, and he'd started to worry they wouldn't come out before his break was over. He didn't care who saw him waiting outside the meeting room in the meantime.

But Ron was emerging, looking self-satisfied until he met Dustin's gaze.

He almost jumped out of his skin, and then gave a quick nod. If there were a way for a grown man to scuttle to his office, that was exactly what he did.

Dustin wasn't surprised to see Glen emerge next, looking flustered. "Ah. Hi, Dustin."

There he was—Leo followed hot on Glen's heels, looking around to find Dustin as he came out. Then he smiled, relaxing at Dustin for just long enough to make Dustin think that maybe…

No. That wasn't good news.

Glen was escorting Leo to his desk.

Dustin nearly dropped his mug. *Oh, fuck.*

He didn't care who had technically fired whom, or who had quit. Unless he was missing some major details, as far as he was concerned, Leo had just been driven out of the department.

"No way," Dustin hissed, falling into step behind Leo.

Glen glanced back at him, then said, "I'll be back in a couple minutes to collect your pass."

Dustin appreciated the moment of privacy, at least. As they reached Leo's desk, he leaned against the cubicle entrance. "No way," he said again. "How did it go down?"

I just got my new boyfriend fired. Somehow. Fuck. How could I have played that differently?

But Leo was smiling. He stepped up to him and rested his hand on Dustin's cheek. "I can do this in the middle of the office now," he murmured.

Dustin blinked at the close contact. Leo was cupping his cheek, gazing just at him, like he was the only thing that mattered. Even though he'd just gotten him fired.

"What's wrong?" Leo asked, his voice quiet.

Dustin shook his head numbly. "You got fired because of me. Or," he raised his hands for air quotes, "quit."

"Fuck, no," Leo shook his head. "You didn't do anything wrong."

If only Dustin could believe that. "I said the wrong thing to Victor, or to Ron… And I dated you. I should have known the rules better than you."

"No," Leo said again, stronger. "This isn't me getting fired. I'm leaving voluntarily, because it became clear near the end of my probationary period that the work environment here doesn't fit me. And yeah, I could have dug in my heels and made them find another reason to fire me, but who needs that shit? I don't." He let go of Dustin and swept the few things on the desk that were his together—the photo frame, a reference book, some snack bars.

Dustin flinched. "Still."

"You didn't make me gay, or make me date you," Leo added, and then winked. "But for the record, it's worth going bi for you."

Dustin tried for a little smile in return. Leo was the one being shunted out; he ought to be supporting *him*.

Leo turned to him again and took his hands. "Dustin, hon. It's the fault of assholes who selectively enforce rules, and of snitches. It's not Victor's, he says, but he seems to know something. I haven't figured out what yet. I would do it all over again for a chance at this." He leaned in to press their lips together.

Dustin kissed Leo back as he slowly started to thaw from the shock. The warm body pressed against him and the hands squeezing his helped. "But what are you gonna do?"

"Joke's on them. I'm gonna be the best damn photographer in the state. I'm gonna give gay couples discounts on their fabulous gay weddings. I'm gonna take photos of trans people to give their families to replace the old family pictures they don't want them to have up around the house. I'm gonna take gay adoption baby photos. All of it," Leo said, his grip almost painfully tight on Dustin's.

Dustin took a deep breath and let it out, then nodded. Leo was a fighter. He would make it through. "I'll... I'll be there with you, of course. But how am I supposed to...?" His voice trailed off as he looked around the office. They were attracting stares from all corners, but he didn't even care right now.

I must be pretty badly shaken if I don't care that I'm the center of attention. Dustin managed a weak smile at the thought.

"There's that beautiful smile," Leo murmured and chuckled. "You're gonna keep doing what you're best at."

Glen was walking up to them. "Guys," he said, his tone suddenly serious. "Hate to break the mood, but a call came in. I've called Paul already. Dustin, you're gonna have your work cut out for you."

"What is it?" Work mode turned on in Dustin's brain.

"Shots fired. We've already got a smoking gun. Looks like domestic violence shit." Glen cursed under his breath. "Lowest of the low. We're hauling the guy in now." He glanced at Leo and shook his head. "I wish we could get you on this, too, man. I'm sorry about how all that went down."

"No, I get it. It was coming from Ron. I could tell," Leo answered, dropping Dustin's hands. "They decided to enforce rules that you didn't care about."

"Yep," Glen said with a dark glare in the direction of HR. "I'm going to be loud about this."

"It's okay," Leo said, shaking his head. "I wanted to get out of here eventually anyway. This just… propelled me."

"Nothing like a swift kick out the door when you've been a good employee," Glen sighed. He looked back at Dustin. "And I'm sorry. For what it's worth, everyone worth his salt in here," another dark glare across the office, "is happy to see you happy."

Dustin managed a slight smile. He didn't really care if people here were happy for him or not after everything that had happened, but Glen's heads-up had stirred something else within him.

"This is how," he said quietly to himself.

Both other men looked at him in confusion.

Dustin cleared his throat and rubbed his forehead, getting his focus back.

It wasn't about the coworkers here, or proving shit to his family, or even to himself. It was the victims… finding justice for them. Even in the midst of an unjust situation, he could make sure *others* got treated fairly. Hell, his work meant the difference between a perp like this guy walking away scot-free or getting a few years cooling their heels behind bars while the victim recovered. If she'd lived.

If not… anger flooded Dustin, but he shut it off.

"I've got work to do." He nodded once to Leo.

"You go be my hero," Leo said softly as he plucked the swipe card from his belt loop and handed it to Glen. "I'll be waiting for you whenever you're done."

While he had him there, a tiny, spiteful, and madly-in-love part of Dustin had an idea. He hauled Leo in for one more abrupt kiss, making damn sure that everyone spying on them had a good chance to see.

They'd see that this wasn't going to break them; it had already done exactly the opposite.

Twenty-Six

LEO

THE WINE GLASS, HALF-FULL, SWIRLED AS LEO NUDGED IT around the coffee table in absentminded circles.

Or was it half-empty?

Leo smiled ruefully to himself, his eyes straying again to the clock above the TV.

It was harder than he'd expected to be patient. He was bursting with decisions, overflowing with the need to share them with someone. And waiting for Dustin to get off work was hell for more than one reason.

Today had been the kind of day he couldn't quite believe had even happened. Was it real? But every time he looked over toward the table where he normally left his key card for the building…

Finally, a knock!

Leo leapt to his feet and nearly sprinted to the front door. When he pulled it open, he barely had time to blink before Dustin was hugging him.

"Hey, baby." Leo wrapped his arms around Dustin and

held him, kicking the door shut with his foot. "You're frozen. It's cold out there?"

"Mm. Parked around the corner. Longer walk than I thought," Dustin mumbled into his shoulder, his grip tight. When he finally relaxed and tipped his chin up for a kiss, Leo got a good look at him. He was tired.

"How was it? Overtime?"

"Yeah, I stayed late. Came straight from work. We got another tip-off, and…" Dustin trailed off, then frowned. "I guess I'm not allowed to talk to you about it now."

Leo sighed and tugged Dustin to the living room. "Can't say I give a shit about their rules right now."

"Me neither. But I think we have the evidence to crucify the guy," Dustin told him, rubbing his chin. "The IT guys are… well, we could have a lot more on him by morning."

"Good," Leo murmured. "You did your job after all that bullshit, and people are going to benefit."

"I did." Dustin managed a little smile, and Leo squeezed his hand. "And I've got tomorrow off. Glen offered."

"I'm proud of you."

Dustin's smile was wider this time. "It sucks. All of this. But the victims are what matter. I know I'm good at this one thing—my job. I can help people."

"Right," Leo agreed. He settled on the couch and pulled Dustin into his lap, wrapping his arms around him.

Dustin glanced at the wine glass, then at him. "Are you okay after all that?"

"Never been better," Leo promised with a smile. "That's my first. Too busy thinking."

"Oh." Dustin breathed out and returned his smile. "Thinking about what?"

Leo chuckled. "Are you ready?"

Dustin slid off his lap so he could face him, slipping his hand into Leo's. "Go for it."

"I'm quitting school and coming out to my parents tomorrow."

"Oh!" Dustin blinked a few times. The owlish look made him look even more tired. "Are those two things related?"

"Not especially," Leo laughed. "But I'm ready to admit what I want—to myself, and to everyone else." Dustin slowly leaned into him, and Leo kissed his temple. "Yes, that means… I want you."

Dustin was blushing and trying to hide it in his shoulder. Then, he stifled a yawn.

Leo chuckled gently. "You're exhausted. Let's get to bed."

Dustin didn't even argue as he steered him up and over to the bedroom. He was quieter than usual, his eyelids heavy as he stripped off and crawled under the covers.

"I don't want to sleep yet," Dustin murmured. "You've had big decisions to make. You must want to talk about that."

Leo shook his head. "It's been a hell of a day. We both need to sleep on it." He pulled Dustin against his chest, shifting around until they found a comfortable position with their limbs entangled but not too heavy on each other.

"My mind's still racing, though," Dustin finally murmured, his cheek against Leo's chest. "Especially after you got… pushed out. It was so fast. It's just so…"

"Yeah. I know," Leo murmured. His chest tightened with frustration and helplessness. A few times that evening, he'd questioned his choice not to fight back. Letting them push him out felt like giving in. "But it's not giving in," he said out loud, half to himself. "I wanted something better for me anyway."

"You don't have to fight every battle that comes your way," Dustin murmured. His fingers ran in slow, soothing circles across Leo's chest and down his side. "Only the ones you want to."

"And I didn't want to fight that one. Not just because it means going public about… well, what I've figured out about myself. But partly that," he admitted. "Hence… coming out. We're dating now. It's none of their business, really. But it'll free me up to say and do whatever I want without waiting for that phone call."

"You mean your new career?"

Leo drew a deep breath and let it out. Thinking about building a business from scratch overnight *was* absolutely terrifying, if he let himself think about it. "Something like that."

"Are you going to be okay, with… rent, or the mortgage?"

"Rent," Leo murmured. "I think so. I have some savings. I'll have to keep an eye on it for the next few months and see how things pan out with new jobs. It'll mean a lot more scrambling for jobs, faster than I thought."

Dustin shifted until his other cheek rested on Leo's chest and he peered up into his face through the semi-darkness of the room. "If you need to move in with me… that could be an option."

The statement made Leo smile, then chuckle.

"What?"

"Thank you for the offer," Leo told Dustin, stroking his hair and running his hand along the back of his neck. "But that was very *you*. Casually dropping it in like that."

"I love you," Dustin said, just as matter-of-factly. "It's an easy choice."

Leo stared at him for a few moments, trying to tell if he

was joking. But he wasn't laughing—just peering back at him, his expression hard to read in this light. "You... do?"

"I know it's pretty quick. But there's something different about you," Dustin said. "And I want to see where that goes. That hasn't happened before. They say you just instantly know? It wasn't instant. I had to think about it and figure out *why* I couldn't figure this out."

"Right," Leo chuckled. "And then you detected traces of love."

"Shut up." Dustin laughed as he flicked Leo's nipple. "Jerk."

"I love you too, you know," Leo told him, wrapping his arms around Dustin and easing him up so he could kiss him.

Dustin kissed back hard, burrowing against him and wrapping his arms and legs around him. When they finally drew apart for breath, Dustin murmured, "So there. If you can't find work fast enough, we'll split costs and make it work. It's half my fault, whatever you say."

"It isn't," Leo grumbled. "It's theirs."

Dustin snorted. "Agree to disagree."

"Oh... and... I'm in that group chat now," Leo told Dustin. "With your brothers."

Dustin made a startled sound. "Really?"

"I asked Josh for help getting work, and then... Roman gave me employment advice, and Falcon started asking around at the bar to see if Victor's been spotted harassing other people, and... it all kind of spun out of control," Leo laughed.

Dustin chuckled, brushing the tip of his nose against Leo's. "That's it. You're adopted now."

Leo couldn't explain how damn warm and fuzzy that made him feel. He swallowed hard and nodded. "It's... It's really nice. Having them around. I see why you like them so much."

"They go to bat for anyone who needs it," Dustin agreed quietly. "What did they find out? About Victor?"

Leo had the worrying feeling that Dustin might do worse than even Leo had considered if he didn't stop this in its tracks. It was always the quiet ones. He didn't want to find out that Dustin had superglued Victor's locker shut or slashed his tires. "I'm still pretty sure he didn't directly cause this."

"Still," Dustin murmured, his eyes closed.

"Um… he doesn't have a great track record with the gay community here," Leo murmured, trying to keep it matter-of-fact. "Neither did his father, when he was sheriff."

"Runs in the family," Dustin muttered. "Typical. And you're sure he didn't report you? Just because you thought you were buddies?"

"You should have seen his face, man. I can't believe I'm defending the guy, but…"

"Neither can I," Dustin admitted, rolling onto his back.

Leo hesitated, then ran his hand up Dustin's arm to his shoulder and turned onto his side to face him. He rubbed his chest tentatively when Dustin didn't pull away. "I'm not choosing him above you. But I don't want to jump on the wrong guy."

"Oh, that's just unfair," Dustin muttered.

"Hm?"

"Appealing to my sense of… fairness," Dustin sighed, looking at him. "Now I can't be mad at him. Or you."

"You can," Leo told him, laughing quietly. "Go ahead. I'm defending a guy who's a dick. That's not very likeable."

"It's lovable but not likeable." Dustin covered Leo's hand

with his, stilling it against his heart. "That's the difference you've taught me."

Leo laughed. "If it just took me being a dick and hanging out with another dick who made you feel like shit in the past, well…"

"When you put it that way it's a bit less loveable. I'd stop now," Dustin advised him, but he was laughing.

"I'm sorry, baby." Leo kissed his shoulder. "We'll figure out who has this giant problem with us, and talk to them, and make sure the department fixes its policies so they apply them equally or not at all. Better?"

"Much better," Dustin said. He was still chuckling quietly. He went quiet after a minute and sighed. "Then we get your new business started, and make sure your family also knows we're dating, and we're all set. Right?"

"Until the next disaster," Leo said with a rueful smile.

Dustin yawned and shrugged, rolling onto his side and scooting back until he pressed against Leo's chest. "That's life."

Leo wrapped his arm around Dustin, rubbing his chest gently as he threw one leg over his. "That's life," he echoed. "Now, get some sleep."

At last, Dustin didn't complain. He nodded slightly, his hand resting over Leo's. "Good night, love."

Leo's chest burned with warmth and appreciation for the incredible man who chose to be by his side. "Good night," he murmured and kissed the back of Dustin's neck. "I love you, too."

After all that, tonight wasn't the right time to tell Dustin what he suspected. It was nothing solid, just a hypothesis… but it made sense. He lay awake for minutes after Dustin's breathing had evened out into a regular rhythm.

But with the brothers at their backs, he and Dustin could do this. One way or another, they had to. No matter where the road led, there was no turning back.

CHAPTER
Twenty-Seven

LEO

"IT'LL BE OKAY."

"Sure it will," Leo murmured, squeezing Dustin's hand back as he waited for his mom to answer the door.

There weren't many more dramatic ways of coming out: walking in holding hands with another man. On the other hand, it was the easiest way to get it out of the way as quickly as possible.

Everything could go really weird in about ten seconds' time, and it was way too late to turn back. Dustin's grip on his hand was firm. He wasn't letting Leo let go, and Leo was grateful for it. Sometimes he wondered how Dustin could squeeze all that damn bravery into his slender frame. He felt like half the man Dustin was right now. Dustin could surely feel his hand shaking.

The door was opening. "Leo! There you are, darling," his mother greeted, then paused, looking confused as she noticed Dustin—and the death-grip Leo had on his hand.

He could see the recognition dawning in her eyes. Aside from holidays, he didn't come home much, so he'd only seen them once since moving to town. Getting a call from him, asking he could come over and talk to them, had to have been a surprise. This explained it all as simply as he could.

"Hey, Mom." Leo swallowed hard and smiled as he stepped inside, leading Dustin. "Is Dad home?" His step-dad had gotten the title sometime in elementary school, just because calling his father figure Rob raised questions he hadn't always wanted to answer.

"Yes, of course. Hon. There's someone to meet." His mom's tone was significant.

Rob came in from the living room, and as expected, he noticed them holding hands before he even reached them. His brows furrowed in confusion. "Leo?"

"Hey, Dad. This is Dustin, my boyfriend." Leo tried to speak casually yet confidently. The balance was suddenly hard to find. "Dustin, my mom and dad."

"Hi, Mrs. Sanderson. Mr. Sanderson," Dustin greeted, letting go of Leo's hand to shake.

Rob let him, looking somewhat dazed. "Leo," he said again. "Dustin. Right."

"I guess we should talk," Leo said, nodding toward the living room.

Dustin breathed out a quick sigh and bent over to take his shoes off as Leo did the same, probably thinking the same thing: *at least they're inviting us in to talk.*

Jesus. Leo shook his head and settled on the couch, patting the spot next to him for Dustin to join him. The tension in the room was even worse than it had been at Dustin's parents' place.

"So, uh. How long has this been going on? Have you been dating?" His mom corrected herself after a moment, perhaps thinking that sounded a little accusatory.

"Just since the weekend. I wanted you guys to know before the rumor mill and the grapevine got to work," Leo smiled.

Dustin sat straight, hands in his lap. He didn't say much, but he was closely watching Leo's parents. Leo just prayed they weren't about to be jerks in front of him. He didn't really want to get the same *you don't deserve that* speech he'd had to give Dustin himself not long ago.

"Right," Rob said, settling back in his recliner and folding his hands against his stomach as he looked between them. "We didn't know you were... dating men now."

Leo shook his head. "It's pretty new to me, too. I never really thought about dating much. You remember how I was," he said with a quick smile. "Focused on my career. After I left the military, I started to think about dating. Moved back here, and... well, I kept meaning to sign up for an app or something. But then we ran into each other, and..." He shrugged, as unable to explain it to them as he had been to himself. "I realized it's not just women who I'm interested in. Dustin stood out right away."

"So it's not all men..." his mother started.

Leo laughed. "Not every single man in Knoxville. Don't worry, Mom. I don't have that much free time." That made her blush and reconsider her next words—long enough for him to get more in edgewise. "Men in general, yes. Women, yes. I'm bi. I never really thought about it, because I knew I liked women."

"Right," Rob dragged out the syllable for a second. "And this phase..."

"Not a phase," Leo interrupted, trying to stay patient. "Do you mean this discovery, or this relationship? Choose one."

He paused, looking between them for a moment. "This...

self-discovery, if you like. Is that just since you were discharged?"

Leo nodded. "Pretty much. I mean, I noticed men before. I just thought it was…" He had to choose his words careful. *Normal* was still a little too quick to come to mind. That wasn't right at all. Too many years not thinking about this shit. "Straight guy bonding stuff," he chose instead.

"Do you think it could be… your experiences in war zones?" Rob asked.

Leo cast them a confused look.

"Some trauma response," his dad clarified.

Leo laughed and groaned at the same moment as he heard Dustin gasp. He rubbed his forehead and shook his head. Of course his dad would want to relate it to the military—and something broken in him, instead of something still precious and whole and growing every day.

"A lot of men in uniform get home and figure out new things about themselves," Dustin interjected. "Everything they were running away from when they enlisted. It doesn't mean being overseas *caused* it."

Leo glanced at Dustin quickly. "Yeah. That's a good way of putting it, I guess."

"So you were running from… us?" Mom asked, her eyes tearing up.

"No, Mom." Leo sighed and rose to his feet, moving over to the loveseat to hug her. "I'm not saying that."

That was half-true. His step-dad, maybe. Not her. Or at least the pressures Rob had put on him from an early age— choosing an active combat career, not girly photography shit. He'd met him halfway, at least.

"I don't understand where this is coming from," she managed, clearing her throat and pushing him away gently as she looked him over, then looked at Dustin. "It's just so sudden."

"It's been sudden for me, too," Leo admitted. "There's been a lot of adjustment. But I'm so damn glad I realized."

"But won't you be happy together?" Rob asked. "If you're… bi, like you say…"

"Bi people can be happy in relationships, sir," Dustin interjected again. "Pardon me for sounding like the gay encyclopedia here. But it's no different from straight people settling down in a relationship. They still find other people attractive, but they choose to date or marry one. Same with bi people—the pool of people they could find attractive is just a little bigger."

Leo shot him a grateful look. "See?" He looked at his dad, then his mom. "I chose the one I love because of who he is, not what he is."

"I still don't think I understand," his mom admitted softly. "But I want to try. You look years younger than you did when you came to see us for Christmas."

Leo crookedly smiled. "I feel it, too. And there's, uh, one other thing." He moved back to the couch to take Dustin's hand again. "We met at work, and some of the officers decided they had a problem with that. Long story short… it was quit or be pushed out on some flimsy excuse. I'm taking my photography freelance. Going to start a small business."

"That's… They fired you because you two are dating?" Rob sat up straight. "Now, hold on. That's not right."

Leo thanked God it worked. Rob was more fired up about his son being mistreated than he was about him being bi. Which automatically brought him around to the side of being okay with him being bi, and the relationship.

Rob seemed to realize it, too. He huffed and shook his head. "That's not right at all."

"We're going to see about getting those rules clarified," Dustin said softly. "They haven't enforced them before, when straight couples in the office got together. And there are married officers—police families. Our supervisor seemed to be on our side."

"But it was a good time for me to make the switch," Leo took over from Dustin, squeezing his hand. "I've been wanting to for a while. Classes in random subjects aren't helping me. This career wasn't, either. Something new and different. Something where I can… I don't know. Show the good side of life again, for the first time in so long. Just normal people being their happy, healthy selves."

His mom nodded slowly. "You've always had that kind of heart. This will make you happier," she said firmly.

Rob couldn't argue. "I suppose so. As long as you've thought about this."

"Oh, I have. There's a lot of work to do, but I can't wait," Leo told them, his lips lifting into a smile. He felt like that represented his relationship with his parents, too. "Speaking of which, we should get going. I just wanted to give you that, and… now some time to process it."

"Okay." His mom rose to her feet and gave him a big hug, followed by Dustin. "Thank you. And it's a pleasure to meet you, Dustin. Where were my manners earlier?"

Dustin's smile was blinding. "Pleasure to meet you, too, ma'am. And… thank you."

CHAPTER
Twenty~Eight
DUSTIN

"Oh, you have got to be kidding."

They weren't even home yet, and the phone was already ringing again. By now, all Dustin wanted was a shower and change of clothes and good, long cuddle with Leo to make the most of his day off work. Enough of this *meeting the parents* bullshit. Hell, neither of them even spoke to their families that much.

What mattered—what was supposed to matter—right now was the two of them.

"Who is it?" Leo asked, frowning at him from the driver's side.

"My parents." Leo snorted, but refrained from comment. Dustin could tell he was trying not to say anything that he wouldn't like to hear about his parents. "I know," Dustin added. "God knows what they want now."

Leo was suddenly busy looking for parking outside Dustin's house.

Dustin hesitated, then answered the phone. "Hey, Mom."

"Hi, sweetpea. Aren't you at work?"

Hearing the affectionate nickname after the tension of that family visit made him smile until he remembered their weekend visit. *Just different kinds of bad.* He'd forgotten how hard it was to come out, it had been so long since he'd done it in family situations, and he'd been so afraid for Leo, unsure of how to help…

"No, I have the day off," he said.

"Well, that's just perfect. You know what? We've got dinner arranged this weekend with one of our friends. You should come by."

Dustin's brow crinkled. *What?* "This… weekend?"

Leo looked at him but didn't comment as he shut off the car.

"Why?" Dustin asked when his mom didn't say anything else. "With whom?"

"With that fellow your father mentioned, the nice accountant."

Dustin shook his head, sliding out of the car now that they were parked. "Why?"

"Your father and I just think you would get along so well."

"Is this… no. I know what this is. He's handsome and single and gay, isn't he?"

"He happens to be, yes," his mom answered, still perky. "But no pressure. If you're free, I'm sure he'd be delighted to meet someone closer to his own age. That's all."

Dustin shut the door harder than he meant to. "And if we happen to fall for each other, so much the better, right?"

"Now, I don't know where this is—"

"Mom. Seriously. You're trying to get me to… what, upgrade? I'm happy with the choices I've made."

"A man with a steady job shouldn't be underrated…" his mom trailed off. "That's all I'm saying."

"He—hang on." Dustin's mind clicked into an awful realization the way some paintings came into focus by stepping back to look at them from twenty feet away. "No. Mom."

"What is it, Dustin?"

"You and Dad… did you call the police department?"

"I don't know anything about that. Dear? Did you call the police this weekend?" she called out. Then she paused. "Certainly not," she concluded.

His father's voice in the background.

"Oh," she added. "We did run into that retired sheriff, Kane Frank. You know, you would have gone to school with his son, Victor."

"And you just so happened to mention that your son was dating a man. Both of whom were employed by a bunch of people who think he's a god," Dustin murmured. He was leaning against the car hood, even though it was warm. He didn't care if he burned his palm—he needed the support.

"Well, we were talking, and it just came up…"

"Mom." Dustin's voice cracked, and Leo was suddenly there by his side, his arm wrapped around his waist. "Mom, he got fired. Or left before they could fire him, whatever. Same difference."

"Oh, honey. That's such a shame." She sounded far less surprised than she should have been, and Dustin's face went as numb as if he'd been slapped.

Leo seemed to have figured it out from his end of the conversation. He drew Dustin away from the hood and into him, supporting his weight as he hugged him.

"No," Dustin muttered into the phone. "That's not good enough. I can't believe you—broke my trust like that. When you're ready to respect me, call me. But I'm not coming to lunch every week to… to give you chances to plant doubts in my mind and find some better guy than him. I love him. Respect me, respect him… or don't talk to me. That's your choice."

Dustin hung up, his hands shaking with anger. He could barely see straight.

"I'm sorry, baby," Leo murmured. "I was starting to suspect… but I didn't know for sure…"

"I thought they were—I didn't think *your* parents would end up being better about it than mine," Dustin mumbled as Leo led him to the house.

"Keys," Leo prompted. On autopilot, Dustin unlocked his door, and Leo steered him inside. "I know," he said once they were inside. "My parents wound up being kind of okay. Confused, but okay."

"And mine tried to get you fired—*did* get you fired. Not because we're gay—bi, same-sex, whatever the word…"

"A blissful romantic partnership between two men," Leo supplied with a gentle smile.

Dustin chuckled and leaned into Leo for a hug, then pulled back to get his jacket and shoes off. "Yeah. Not because of that, but because they think you're not good enough. Well, fuck that and fuck them."

Leo growled under his breath. "I like this Dustin."

"This Dustin is normally kept under wraps," Dustin answered, kicking his stuff to the side and pulling Leo in for another hug. "It's… disconcerting to be this Dustin."

"I love this Dustin as much as every other Dustin," Leo murmured into his hair, his hands rubbing Dustin's back gently. "And I'm sorry your parents aren't respecting you and your choices—still. I can't say it's out of the blue for me, but it has to be a shock for you."

When Dustin was calm enough to think straight, he led

Leo to his room so he could pick out new clothes to change into. Yesterday's were getting old in a hurry. "Thank you for being here through… all that. I'm sorry I wasn't more help with your parents."

"What? No, you were there with me," Leo shook his head. "And you filled in a lot of answers before I could figure out how to phrase them."

"Voice of more experience." Dustin half-smiled at Leo. He picked out a t-shirt and jeans, which was about all he felt like wearing.

"So much more." Leo was watching him with a smile. "Gonna take a shower?"

"I will in a sec." Dustin came back to the bed and sat next to Leo again, leaning into his arm one more time. "Are you sure, though?"

"That you were enough?" As always, Leo cut through the bullshit. "You are, baby."

Dustin wasn't sure he was ready to believe that, but what choice did he have? He drew a breath and let it out, then nodded as he leaned in to hug Leo with all he had.

This had to be enough.

"That explains Victor feeling kind of responsible but not really," Leo murmured after a minute, then tensed up.

Dustin winced. "For what it's worth, I'm sorry I got angry at you for trying to be friends with him."

Leo glanced at him quickly, pulling away to do so. "Are you sure? I mean, I don't *want* to be friends with him anymore. I get why you were pissed off. He was trying to get between us."

"So was everyone. Fuck 'em," Dustin snorted. That attitude was here to stay. "I don't mind that you were friends. I forgive you for hanging out with him instead of me this time around, too. You're not responsible for whatever he or his dad did."

"Thank you for saying that. But I object. Fuck everyone? I prefer to fuck the one gorgeous guy who made me smile throughout all of that," Leo murmured, rubbing his hand down Dustin's arm. "Come on. You know what I want."

Dustin managed a smile for him, and then found himself even laughing at Leo's thumbs-up in response. "I love you, you goof."

"I know you do." Leo winked. "Go on, shower. And then… I have an idea to make the most of our day off. You'll want something nicer than a t-shirt on, though."

"Oh, will I?" Dustin's spirits were creeping slowly up. Goddamn it. How did Leo do it? *Must be love.*

"We're shutting off our phones and going on that date. You know how we said we would? And then life got in the way? Like a clever, gorgeous, sweet man just told me… fuck 'em. Tonight is for us."

A date sounded utterly ridiculous—like hell they could shut off the world after the last few days they'd had. But the more Dustin thought about it, the more perfect it sounded. It *was* exactly what they needed. They had to find a way to leave the rest of it behind somehow, and let it be just them.

Dustin beamed and grabbed a towel. "Be right back."

CHAPTER
Twenty~Nine
LEO

"To beginnings."

Leo clinked his glass against Dustin's. Since they'd been seated, Leo had been unable to take his eyes off him. As Dustin smiled at him, in his face, Leo saw all that he needed.

"What?" Dustin smiled self-consciously.

"Nothing. Except your toast was perfect, and I love you," Leo said with a smile. "And now you're blushing. I was trying to spare you the blush."

Dustin swatted a hand in his direction, laughing. "You're a jerk sometimes."

"Especially before I eat. Sorry I'm so hangry. Or, you might say, hornery…"

"So *wha*—oh. Leo, you can't just say that," Dustin hissed. Even the tips of his ears were red now.

Leo smiled innocently at Dustin before reaching across the table to take his hand. "Oh, fine. I'll be good."

It was nice to do this in public, unafraid of who might be watching. As far as Leo was concerned, anyone who mattered didn't mind and anyone who minded didn't matter.

Dustin seemed skittish at times, but he was coming around to the contact and growing bolder, even in these last few weeks. Leo loved seeing the changes. How much more would Dustin grow while they were together?

"I'm just glad we got to the bottom of that mystery. It's not work talk," Dustin quickly added, grinning at Leo. "Just a general… comment."

Leo gave him a suspicious glance. "Sounds dangerously work-like to me."

"Fine, fine," Dustin grinned. "Pick another subject."

"Am I allowed to say your eyes? I love your eyes. Oooh. The blush is back."

Dustin pulled back from Leo with a laugh and nodded to the side. The waiter was on the way with what looked like their meals. "I have no idea how I'll put up with you."

"None at all?" Leo grinned. He leaned in to murmur, "There are perks."

Dustin made a startled sound but didn't have time to comment before they had to play out the social niceties with the waiter.

When they were alone, Dustin muttered, "Gonna kill you."

"Did that get you feeling a bit too hot to be out in public?" Leo teased. "My apologies. Someone else is hornery, too."

Dustin finally gave in and grinned. "I don't know what I did to deserve you, you know."

"Something terribly bad, or terribly good?" Leo laughed.

"So good I must have had wings," Dustin said, his voice clear and sincere as he gazed at Leo with a shake of his head.

It was Leo's turn to blush, and as Dustin giggled, he rolled his eyes. "I guess I earned that one."

"Yeah. You did. Come on, let's eat up so we can get home."

Leo grinned. "Well, now you're not afraid to ruin the fairytale, are you?"

As Dustin started eating, he glanced over his glass once more at Leo. "I finally realized it wasn't going away."

"That's right, baby." Leo watched him with a broad smile.

The way Dustin sparkled under his attention was captivating. He even chattered when Leo let him, carried away by moments of excitement he rarely let shine through at work or out with groups. This was another side of Dustin he only saw one-on-one, and Leo wanted to cover it in bubble wrap.

But Dustin was resilient, too—strong enough to make it through the worst kind of betrayal and still look radiantly beautiful over supper that night. Fuck the military macho bullshit—Leo hoped he could be half the man Dustin was, alone in his lab studying computer images late at night.

"What?" Dustin prompted again.

"Sorry," Leo grinned, realizing he hadn't even started eating. "Got carried away with my fairytale, too."

Dustin nudged his foot. "Glad you stalked me?"

"I what? I did not!" Leo protested around a bite of food.

"You sure did. That first gift card? Note under the door? *Unsigned* note?" Dustin teased. "That's pretty stalkery."

Leo groaned as the memory hit him, and Dustin laughed again. "Okay," Leo conceded. "A little. But gimme a break. I'd never dated anyone. How was I supposed to know?"

Dustin set down his utensils for a sip of wine, watching Leo sharply. "Never?"

Leo's cheeks flushed. Somehow, it seemed like less of a big deal now, after all they'd been through. He shook his head. "I've gone on dates, sure. Looked at attractive people. But... an actual relationship? You were my first, baby."

"You didn't say." Dustin was smiling warmly.

"No." Leo cleared his throat and dabbed his mouth, avoiding his gaze for a moment. "Uh, I was… worried what you'd think… worried I didn't know what I was doing… worried about all of it."

"You're a natural, then," Dustin told him. "I'll give you all the practice you need."

Leo grinned. "In every way, I'm sure. I know it'll be a sacrifice, but you'll just have to manage."

"My pleasure," Dustin winked and sipped his wine, giving Leo a sultry look.

Leo couldn't resist murmuring, "There'll be lots of that." The look on Dustin's face as he tried not to cough with a mouthful of wine was so worth it.

Everything else might be uncertain, even scary, but that was life. It was worth it to have a man across the table from him, glowing like the sun with love and affection and curiosity about him. Leo closed his eyes for a moment to bask in the feeling.

Dustin was the focal point of his life. Now that Leo had found him, everything else was slowly coming into the sharpest focus he'd ever known.

Thirty

DUSTIN

"I can't believe that Uber had mints in the backseat! And travel Scrabble! I wonder if it had travel packs of lube, for the inconvenient moments?"

"We've gone from hornery to horny," Leo laughed.

"No. Maybe." Dustin almost fell over Leo as they hurried inside and out of the damn cold evening. The cold snap had snuck up while they were in the restaurant. His jacket suddenly wasn't quite enough to stay warm.

"I think I've taken so many cars in the last couple months—especially the last month, and I'm not sure whose fault *that* is," Leo said sternly, tapping Dustin's nose before letting him by. "That they've upgraded my star rating to unlock, like, the fanciest drivers."

Dustin giggled. "It's definitely not my fault." He moved in to nip Leo's finger, but Leo whipped his hand away too fast.

"Hm. Bad boy," Leo slapped his ass and closed the door.

Dustin moaned, then licked his lips. "Oh, good evening to you, too."

Leo grinned. "It's a good thing I like my men sassy."

"It's a good thing I wasn't trying," Dustin retorted.

"Neither was I." Leo waggled his brows. When Dustin turned to ditch his coat and bent over to take off his shoes, Leo smacked his ass again, a little harder.

"Oof!" Dustin hadn't been expecting that, but Leo's other hand rested on Dustin's hip to keep him steady on his feet. He wiggled his ass in the air and then straightened up to grind against Leo. "Turns out I like it when you try."

"I'll remember that. And I believe we have something to celebrate. Other than... well, us," Leo murmured. He wrapped his arms around Dustin's waist, his hands sliding up his shirt and down his pants at the same time.

Dustin giggled and squirmed with pleasure as broad, warm palms ignited his nerves. "What's that?"

"Our test results," Leo smiled. "If you're interested in bareback. If not, no sweat."

Dustin turned his head to the side to catch Leo's lips, not caring about the awkward angle. "I am," he murmured. "Are you gonna fuck me hard and leave me wet?"

"Jesus," Leo gasped. Dustin could feel his cock reacting to that, hardening against his ass. He loved tempting and teasing his boyfriend, just as he had been all night.

"Gonna fill me up with that sexy boner I feel?" Dustin hummed, reaching behind his head to catch the back of Leo's head and rub his neck, pulling his head down to kiss his neck.

Leo mouthed behind his ear. "You're so much trouble."

"I'm *in* so much trouble? Or I *am*?" Dustin squirmed again, rocking his hips back and forth until Leo groaned.

"Both." Leo unbuttoned Dustin's shirt while groping his cock through his underwear with the other. In the confined space, the extra pressure felt heavenly.

"Oh! Fuck, yes," Dustin groaned. "I'm going to keep getting into trouble if this is what it gets me."

"This and so much more," Leo promised. He nudged Dustin hard enough that Dustin realized he was walking him in the direction of his bedroom.

Dustin resisted for a moment more to really grind their bodies together, then giggled and let Leo steer them. "All night long, huh?"

"All night long, if that's what you want."

"I want you," Dustin whispered, his smile growing at how damn true it was. "I want you so much."

All his worries and fears seemed like silly hangups when Leo was there with him. Prince Charming could bend him over and screw him, and he wouldn't screw him over afterward. It wasn't just chemistry. It was… caring. Kindness. The guys Dustin had found before were not this man.

Though this man was sure stripping their clothes off at the speed of light.

"Oh, I wasn't the only horny one at that restaurant," Dustin grinned. He watched as Leo stepped out of his trousers and socks, cursing under his breath. "Not judging by that sexy cock of yours."

"You were having the same problem, weren't you?" Leo retorted, smirking. "We're really as bad as each other."

Dustin laughed as he tumbled onto the bed and pulled Leo after him. "We are. And I love that."

Their bodies were warm and smooth together as Leo straddled him, legs touching from feet to thighs, stomachs touching, his head bending down toward him…

And then they kissed, warm and wet and passionate. Their tongues slid together, Leo's lips catching Dustin's as he sucked until Dustin moaned.

"I love you," Leo whispered against his mouth, so softly that Dustin wondered if he'd imagined it. But that look was very much real—the look that told him Leo adored him.

Dustin's body was already burning. His cheeks had to be, too. "I love you, too. I'm so damn glad you stalked me."

"Hey!" Leo pouted in protest.

Dustin laughed and kissed him until that expression was replaced with bliss once more. "Grab the lube."

"Wasting no time, are we?" Leo grinned.

"There's time for blowjobs and cuddling later." Dustin slid up the bed until Leo's hard cock was nestled between his thighs, then squeezed them together.

Leo's hips jerked and he thrust a few times, then moaned into Dustin's neck. "I see your point."

Dustin let him go, laughing as he watched him scramble for the bottle. He stole it from Leo's hand and cracked it open himself, grinning at the expression on Leo's face. "You never knew you wanted this show, huh?"

"Oh, I imagined it," Leo murmured, his voice husky. "So many times."

Dustin spread his legs and slid two wet fingers inside himself, his other hand jerking his cock slowly. "So do I. I've done this before, thinking about you sliding into me. Imagining the next time I'd get to feel your big, hard dick so deep inside me."

Leo's expression was a priceless mix of embarrassment, pride, and lust. He swallowed hard, like he was reminding himself how to talk. "I... Fuck. Dustin."

"Yes. You fuck Dustin now," Dustin teased.

Leo laughed richly, throwing back his head. His throat exposed, Dustin leaned in to kiss it a few times. Leo moaned and held the position for a few moments before kissing him again.

"If you're sure," Leo whispered, his cock head nudging at the entrance.

Dustin smiled. "So damn sure."

Thick warmth slid inside, but it was nothing compared to the warmth in his chest. Meeting Leo's eyes the whole time, watching Leo's expression tighten with pleasure, hearing him gasp as Dustin enveloped him…

It was priceless.

"And maybe next round, I'll take another turn on top," Dustin hummed. "See how much you've been practicing for me."

Leo moaned sharply. "God, yes. We have all night. Except…"

"I can show up at work sleepless for once. And preferably covered in hickeys. Serves 'em all fucking right," Dustin told Leo, grinning.

Leo laughed as he eased inside Dustin, his gaze focused on the point where their bodies met and melded. "Oh, fuck. You feel so good."

Dustin's response was lost in a moan as Leo started moving in and over him. The muscles of his forearms rippled on either side of Dustin's head as Leo braced himself for short, shallow thrusts that gradually deepened.

If I didn't know he was so damn honest, Dustin thought, *I'd be pretty sure he was lying about me being his first guy. He's a natural in every way.*

Their lips met again and time itself seemed to disappear. There was only Leo, groaning Dustin's name into the air like a prayer, and Dustin, rising from the pillow to meet Leo's lips with kisses before Leo pressed him down again.

Dustin tried his hardest to hold out. When Leo reached for his cock, he brushed his hand away with a breathless laugh. "You first."

"Are you sure? I'm sure that's how I met you." Leo grinned down at him, his voice breathless.

Dustin laughed. "And thank God for that." He ran his hands up Leo's sides to his shoulders. "I want to feel you. Come for me, baby."

Leo thrust harder and faster, hitting the prostate with every thrust and lighting up every inch of Dustin's skin with pleasure. Hell, if Leo kept this up for long, he was going to come, even if his cock was trapped between their stomachs and rubbing maddeningly gently.

"Dustin, baby—"

"I love you. Let me feel you come," Dustin whispered, kissing Leo's cheeks and lips. "You're mine. Make me yours."

"Yes!" Leo managed, and then he was beyond himself with pleasure. His hips jerked forward, and fuck, Dustin loved that rough, hard pace.

Dustin hastily worked a hand between them both to jerk himself off. He was so close. Too close. He needed release, and he needed it now.

He spilled over the edge seconds later, crying out wordlessly as he squirmed under Leo and squeezed around his softening cock.

"I loved that," Leo whispered as he slid out, peppering Dustin's forehead and cheeks with kisses. "I love *you*."

"I love you, too, baby," Dustin mumbled once he could think straight, laughing as he swatted at Leo. "Hey, you. Give me a second to breathe."

Leo grinned and settled for kissing his shoulder instead as he rolled onto his side next to him. "I thought you wanted all the romance you could handle. I'll just kiss you more later to make up for it."

"You'd better," Dustin grinned. Now that his senses were coming back to him as his cock softened, he managed to roll onto his side facing Leo. He leaned in to return all those kisses with just one of his own: soft, lingering, and as sweet as could be. "Hey. You came. My very own Prince Charming."

Little lines crinkled around Leo's eyes when he smiled this hard. "And they lived happily ever after, no doubt."

Dustin grinned and nodded. He heard exactly what Leo was telling him, and it made his heart sing. "Yeah? Beyond a reasonable doubt?"

Leo ran his thumb along Dustin's jaw until he cupped his cheek. After one more kiss, he whispered, "Not even a trace of doubt."

"As some of you guys know, I wrote that song because of one man."

Here it was. Leo's finger rested on the shutter button, his focus already set. He knew where it was going to happen—the mark had already been laid in tape on the stage. So did the lighting guys, and most of the crew, actually.

How the hell everyone had kept the secret so well, Leo didn't know.

But he'd gotten pretty good at photographing people again over these last few months, as quickly as the brothers had found work for him. Thank God, because this was a night he didn't want to mess up.

"And now that I'm playing in my hometown, I get to really embarrass him. Come on up, Nico." Deen gestured with a finger, curling it to beckon Nico up. He was grinning as he shielded his gaze to get a look at the front row where his boyfriend—and all their friends—sat.

Leo was snapping photos every few seconds leading up to the big moment.

"I've also got a bunch of my friends here tonight. These guys are incredible. The kind of guys who would give the shirts off their backs. Aw, don't blush, guys. I won't make you come up here. Just stand up and give a wave. That's it."

Leo grinned to himself. Dustin would be dying of embarrassment right about now.

"And one more guy, the one who's been scooting back and forth here all night—our wonderful event photographer —he's part of the group, too."

Deen was talking to fill the time until Nico made it up to the stage, Leo was pretty sure. He was going red himself with the eyes of a crowd of thousands on him, but he just gave a quick wave and went back to photographing Nico climbing up onto the stage.

"All of them are phenomenal. They've reminded me how important family is. Whether that's born or chosen family, doesn't matter. The people who have your back."

And had they ever. Throughout the last few months, a careful word in people's ears had returned results. They'd found out and relayed to Leo that a handful of complaints against Victor for discrimination in the last few years had been mysteriously dropped after Victor's dad intervened.

But Victor had promised to change, and so far, he actually had. Whatever had prompted his change of heart, he'd been willing to openly admit that he'd confirmed to his dad that the two of them were dating, and he'd even said—to both of them—how bad he felt about it.

Apparently, knowing a bi guy made him think twice about the stuff his dad said, and then... well, he'd realized he was being a dick.

They were never going to be friends—not like Leo was

friends with the brothers now, practically a brother himself —but at least they weren't enemies.

And the photography business was going fine. A couple of straight police officers had even approached Leo, asking for family photos or wedding photos or engagement photos. They'd wanted to show support as HR reviewed its policies. The tide felt like it was turning.

The audience was cheering and clapping now.

Nico joined Deen now, eyes down as he stepped over wires to the empty spot on the stage, marked only by the tape X. Did he suspect? If so, he didn't show it. Turned out the park ranger who gave small press conferences now had been an astronaut before, used to way bigger press conferences and photo ops. He handled the stage okay, though he was looking at Deen more than the audience.

"And nobody has had my back more than Nico. My boyfriend. Come here, babe." Deen planted a kiss on Nico's lips while people hooted and hollered. "If it weren't for him, man. I don't know where I'd be. When he agreed to come up on stage, he had no idea what he was in for, guys."

The audience went silent now and Nico glanced over at Deen, looking startled.

Carefully, Leo documented every expression, moving around to capture angles of both of them. Exactly when they'd planned it, Deen dropped to one knee.

Nico looked confused at first. Then, at last, it hit him. He gasped, covering his mouth with both hands.

The *awww* from the audience, and even Deen's words—it all faded to a distant murmur as Leo focused on snapping photos.

"The man who's made me whole, who showed me the sky

and kept me grounded… you *are* the smoke on my mountains, the North Star in my sky. Would you make me the happiest man alive and be my husband?"

Only years of training kept Leo's eyes dry as he photographed Nico nodding *yes*, and Deen's expression shifting from nervous and tentative hope to delight.

Deen sliding the ring onto Nico's finger, the dimmed lights overhead glinting off the metal.

Nico rose to his feet, grabbing Deen and kissing him while the audience cheered—none louder than the guys in the front row, right behind Leo.

He didn't let himself tear up until it was over, Nico back in his seat and Deen singing the next song. Finally, Leo rejoined the guys in the front row for a few minutes.

"You guys all knew," Nico hissed, leaning over them.

They grinned back smugly.

"You're all secretive little fuckers. God." Nico wiped his eyes again. "The lights. Really bright up there."

"Uh huh. They were pretty bright down here, too," Leo teased.

Dustin took his hand and squeezed. "Relax and enjoy the rest of the set," he said. "You've done your job."

So Leo stayed with him, only letting go of his hand to clap. His face hurt from grinning by the end of the evening, when everyone else had filed out and Deen had emerged from his dressing room ready for a wild celebration. And what a well-documented kind of wild celebration it was.

The best kind of all, because Dustin was there, and everyone was happy. Even for those without boyfriends or fiancés, brotherly love was never far away. Looking at his photos at the end of the night, Leo had to wipe his eyes one more time before he joined Dustin in bed.

Turned out he could capture love on camera.
Who knew?

Clutch

SIGNIFICANT BROTHERS #5

"HE'S FLIRTY, DIRTY, AND STUBBORN AS HELL. HOW CAN I RESIST?"

Cocky racing driver Tyler Joseph is sidelined after a fiery crash forces him to rest and recover at his best friend's farmhouse. If he ignores the doctor's orders, he might miss the rest of the season.

Tyler does what he wants, though, and what he wants right now is the hot, sexy little physical therapist whose hands only touch him where it hurts.

Alec Lands promised himself he'll stop dating trouble, but he's a sucker for a pretty face, and Tyler is too much temptation to bear. Finally, he gives in—on the condition that it's a one-time thing. They both know it could end their careers.

But they can't stop, no matter how hard they try. Every risk they take could end them forever... but Alec wants to keep up with Tyler's fast-paced life, and Tyler is tired of leaving men in the dust.

When they're sent into a tailspin, it'll take everything they have to reach their destination: forever, together. Will they hit the brakes too soon—or, worst of all, too late?

Also by E. Davies

Sunrise Island Brothers:

Collide

Stranded

Hart's Bay:

Hard Hart

Changed Hart

Wild Hart

Stolen Hart

Significant Brothers:

Splinter

Grasp

Slick

Trace

Clutch

Tremble

Riley Brothers:

Buzz

Clang

Swish

Crunch

Slam

Grind

Brooklyn Boys:

Electric Sunshine

Live Wire

Boiling Point

F-Word:

Flaunt

Freak

Faux

Forever

Freedom

After:

Afterburn

Afterglow

Aftermath

Shared Universes:

Shelter

Adore

Miracle

Redemption

Limelight

Barely Regal

www.ingramcontent.com/pod-product-compliance
Lightning Source LLC
Chambersburg PA
CBHW050842190726

48286CB00007B/2186